P9-DDB-789

Failure to Return
Library Material
is a crime
N. C. General
Statues# 14-398

# UNGIFTED

# UNGIFTED

## GORDON KORMAN

BALZER + BRAY

*An Imprint of* HarperCollins*Publishers*

Balzer + Bray is an imprint of HarperCollins Publishers.

Ungifted
Copyright © 2012 by Gordon Korman
All rights reserved. Printed in the United States of America.
No part of this book may be used or reproduced in any manner whatsoever
without written permission except in the case of brief quotations embodied
in critical articles and reviews. For information address HarperCollins
Children's Books, a division of HarperCollins Publishers,
10 East 53rd Street, New York, NY 10022.
www.harpercollinschildrens.com

Typography by Erin Fitzsimmons
13  14  15  16   CG/RRDH   10  9  8  7

First Edition

*For the highly gifted Lev Jensen Iserson*

*And special thanks to Coach John "Motch"
Motchkavitz and the award-winning
Great Neck South High School
Robotics Team #2638*

# UNEARTHED

## DONOVAN CURTIS
## IQ: 112

I want a refund from ancestry.com.

They traced my family all the way back to the revolution. And in all those forefathers and foremothers, aunts, uncles, and cousins, there was nobody like me. No bigmouth hung for treason; no "classe clowne" who they stuck in the stocks and threw rotten vegetables at. The closest match was this guy in the Civil War who jumped off a battlement, whatever that is. And he only did it because the Union army was firing on Fort Sumter. That's what they put on his tombstone anyway. It sounds like a pretty good excuse to me.

I did things like that. If there were any battlements in my neighborhood, I'd probably jump off them all. And not because of any army. I'd do it just to see what would happen. "Reckless," my mother called me. "Poor impulse control." That's the school psychologist. "You're going to break your idiot neck one day, or someone's going to break it for you." My dad.

He was probably right. They were all right. But when the *thing* is right there in front of me, and I can kick it, grab it, shout it out, jump into it, paint it, launch it, or light it on fire, it's like I'm a puppet on a string, powerless to resist. I don't think; I *do*.

It can be little things, like throwing darts at a pool float to test my sister's swimming skills, or spitting back at the llamas at the zoo. It can be more creative—a helium balloon, a fishhook, and Uncle Mark's toupee. It can even be the smart-alecky comments that got me voted Most Likely to Wind Up in Jail in my middle school the last two years running.

"Our fans are great; our team is nifty! We're going to get blown out by fifty!"

See, that was probably not the wisest thing to say

on the day of the big game against our basketball archrivals, Salem Junior High. But I didn't just say it; I broadcast it over the PA system to the entire school. I don't know why I did it. The cheer was already fully formed in my mind—the poster advertising the big game had planted it there. It was definitely going to come out. Why share it with only the two Daniels, who were with me in the office awaiting sentence for our spitball war, when there was a perfectly good microphone a few feet away, unattended and live. Okay, it wasn't live. I had to flick the switch. I even had pom-poms—well, a crumpled piece of paper for sound effects.

The howl of protest that went up all around the building surprised even me. It was like I'd gone from house to house, poisoning everybody's dog. It was probably for my own good that I wound up in detention. If I'd been free in the halls at three-thirty, I would have been lynched. The sense of humor at Hardcastle Middle School didn't extend to their precious basketball team.

"Why'd you say we're going to lose, man?" asked Whelan Kaiser, starting center, peering down at the top of my head from his six-foot-four vantage.

Why? There was no logical explanation for what

I did. It had to come from my DNA. That's why I needed ancestry.com.

I was the only kid in detention that afternoon. All crimes had been forgiven in order to pad the audience for the big game against Salem, which had to have already started. All crimes except mine—dissing the basketball team. Even the Daniels—two-thirds of the spitball war—had been cut loose while I was doing time.

The Daniels weren't at the game. I knew this because they were skulking in the bushes outside the detention room, making grotesque faces at me through the window. If they could make me laugh—and it wasn't easy to hold back—I'd be in even more trouble. As it was, Mr. Fender was checking his watch every thirty seconds. He wanted to be at the game, not babysitting me.

Finally, he could bear it no longer. "I'll be right back," he told me sternly.

The instant he was gone, the window was flung open from the outside.

"Come on!" hissed Daniel Sanderson. "Let's get out of here!"

"He's coming back," I protested.

"No, he's not," scoffed the other Daniel—Daniel

Nussbaum. "He's going to the office to watch the feed from the security camera in the gym. You've only got ten more minutes. If he's any kind of basketball fan, you're golden."

I was out the window like a shot, breathing sweet, free air. See what I'm saying? The open road called, and I took it. This time I'd needed a little help. That's where the Daniels came in. They helped me a lot. They'd helped me to the office with our spitball fight, and helped me to the PA mic by daring me to do it. With friends like them, sometimes I wondered why I would ever need enemies.

I turned on them. "Thanks for letting me take the fall alone. Your support was really touching."

Nussbaum shrugged innocently. "I couldn't take credit for your poem."

"It wasn't a poem. It just happened to rhyme."

"I've been meaning to talk to you about that," Sanderson put in. "Don't you think that's kind of dorky? I mean, who rhymes anymore?"

"Nobody," I conceded, "except the entire hip-hop community." I bounced a pinecone off his head, which only made him grin wider.

We were at the top of the hill, looking down on the gym we shared with Hardcastle High. The parking lot was jam-packed. A roaring cheer spilled out of the building.

"Man, you couldn't fit a Hot Wheels car in there!" Nussbaum exclaimed, taking in the crowded lot. "Salem-*vs.*-Hardcastle is the place to be."

"Let's go check out the score," said Sanderson. "We can see if our 'nifty' team will lose by 'fifty.'"

"Yeah, Donovan, nice school spirit," Nussbaum added. Like *he* had any.

We started down, the Daniels jostling each other absently. A kind of friendly belligerence came naturally to those two. Maybe they were descended from the Hatfields and the McCoys. I'll bet the Daniels had never checked it out on ancestry.com.

And then The Moment was upon me.

I must have passed the statue of Atlas a thousand times going back and forth on the campus of the Hardcastle Public Schools. Yet somehow it was like I'd never seen it before.

It was not the titan's broad powerful shoulders supporting the bronze globe of the world and heavens that seemed so different. But since when did Atlas have such a big butt? Seriously, I knew he was a titan; but I didn't know that the most titanic thing about him was his caboose. He looked like a reject from *The Biggest Loser.*

Suddenly, I was striding toward the statue, in an almost trancelike state. I picked up a fallen tree branch and made my approach.

Nussbaum noticed my zombielike concentration. "Dude, what are you doing?"

I didn't answer, and he didn't really expect me to. He knew me. They both did.

I cocked back the branch, and unloaded a home run swing. The impact vibrated up through my arms to my brain stem, and into every cell of my body. The branch shattered in my hands.

I have to say that this was always the best part of it for a guy like me—the split second the tomato hits the car; the very brief flight as I drop from the edge of the roof to the pool; the instant that the balloon lifts the toupee and the sun's rays glint off that shiny bald head.

Or, in this case, the *go-o-o-ong!* sound from the statue's bronze behind. The payoff. It was usually downhill from there. Sometimes literally.

Atlas shivered as the vibration traveled through his metal body. The celestial sphere shivered too, rocking dizzily on his muscular shoulders. At that point, I noticed for the first time that the sculpture wasn't a single piece of metal, but two, bolted together at the nape of the titan's neck.

Corrosion is a terrible thing. It was all in slow motion, but there was nothing you could do to stop it. With a crack, the bolt snapped, pieces whizzing out of sight. The ball of the world and heavens toppled and hit the ground with a *whump!*

I was still wrapped up in The Deed, lost in The Moment. It took the twin gasps from the Daniels to break the trance. And by that time, the heavy ball was already rolling.

Oh, no . . .

The big bronze globe careened down the hill toward the gym, picking up speed as it went. I ran after it, although what I thought I could do to stop it, I have no idea.

"Help me!" I called to the Daniels. But they were heading in the opposite direction. They liked to watch me do stuff; they had a lot less interest in hanging around for the consequences.

Heart sinking, I projected the course of the runaway globe. The prognosis was not good. It was hurtling straight for the parking lot, where a lot of innocent cars were waiting to get bashed in. Desperately, I threw myself headfirst at the juggernaut. When my shoulder struck the heavy metal, it felt like running into a brick wall. If it changed the direction at all, it was about a millionth of an inch. Flat on my face now, all I could do was watch.

The globe screamed down toward all that expensive machinery, bounced off an upturned curbstone, and caromed toward the building. The cars were safe, but the world and heavens were now on a collision course with the basketball game.

It pulverized the glass doors, sending up a blizzard of shards that obscured the entrance. I heard a very sharp whistle blast, like the referee was calling a foul on Atlas, or possibly me.

There was another relative on ancestry.com. He wasn't very much like me. I doubt I would have remembered him at all, except for his name—James Donovan. I'd wondered if I was named after him, although my mother claimed she'd never heard of the guy. He emigrated from Ireland in 1912, which would have been fine except that the ship he picked was— think Atlas here—the *Titanic*.

As decision makers, he and I were pretty much on the same level.

But get this: He didn't die. He was plucked from the freezing water alive.

James Donovan was a *survivor*.

If I'd inherited any of those skills, I had a sinking feeling they were about to come in handy.

# UNIDENTIFIED

## DR. SCHULTZ
## IQ: 127

To be the superintendent of a school district like Hardcastle, with its forty-seven buildings and more than thirty thousand students, was a huge responsibility. A lot of administrators would have hundreds of complicated rules to follow. I only had one: No screwups.

So when I took time out of my busy schedule and burdensome duties to attend a middle school basketball game, I expected to see orderly students, good sportsmanship, and happy alumni. What I did *not* expect to see was a giant metal ball blasting into the gymnasium, scattering players like tenpins. Not only did it create a dangerous situation, but it also reflected very badly on the Hardcastle schools.

Miraculously, no one was injured. Still, there was a lot of chaos as the parents of the players rushed to their sons on the floor in an effort to protect them from whatever this onslaught was.

I knew instantly. That globe was part of the statue of Atlas that stood on the knoll overlooking the school. And it certainly hadn't rolled itself down to the gym. I raced through the shattered door and onto the lawn. I could see the ribbon of crushed grass all the way back to the figure of Atlas, who looked peculiar, bent under the weight of absolutely nothing.

The culprit lay in the flattened path, raised up on his elbows, staring at the damage, guilty. "You, there!" I called.

The boy tried to scramble up and run, but he couldn't get any traction on the squashed turf. By the time he found his feet, I was upon him, and he was caught.

"Come with me to my office."

His shoulders slumped. "Yeah, okay." He looked as worried as he ought to be. I drew some small satisfaction from that.

The administration building was on the very same campus, but the boy didn't speak on the way over, not even to protest his innocence. A fat lot of good that would have done him. I had him dead to rights. And the evidence—a four-hundred-pound bronze sphere, and the damage it had caused—spoke plainly about what he had done.

At last, we reached my office, and I glared at him across my desk. "Do you know who I am?"

He shook his head, and had the grace to look a little scared.

"I am Dr. Schultz, Superintendent of the Hardcastle Independent School District. And I'll have your name and your school's name right now."

"Donovan Curtis. I go here—I mean Hardcastle Middle, where, uh, *it* happened."

I wrote the information on a piece of paper on the cluttered desk in front of me. "Well, Donovan Curtis, I don't have to tell you that you're in big trouble right now. You're lucky that no one was hurt or even killed by that stunt of yours. Why would you do such a thing?"

"It was an accident."

If he thought he could get away with an excuse like that, he had picked the wrong administrator. "A giant metal ball doesn't plow through a building by accident."

He spoke up again. "I hit the statue with a branch, but I didn't think the world would fall off."

"You didn't think—"

My secretary, Mrs. De Bourbon, came bustling in, looking worried. "I'm so sorry to disturb you, Dr. Schultz, but you're needed urgently back at the gym. Someone called the fire department from a cell phone, and you're the only one with the authority to send them away." She frowned. "Nothing's on fire, is it?"

"No, of course not." I was halfway to the door when I hesitated. What to do with the boy? He was looking hopeful, as if he were home free. But believe me, he wasn't. It would serve him right if I left him sitting here, cooling his heels, while I went out to deal with the mess he'd made! But who knew how long that would take? By now those firefighters could be finding code violations in the gym! And I had a dinner meeting across town. . . .

I skewered him with my most severe expression. "You can go. I'll send for you tomorrow morning, and we can continue this discussion."

He was out of there like a shot. I wasn't far behind him when Mrs. De Bourbon called me back.

"I'm sorry to bother you again, but Student Services needs the list of the new candidates for the gifted program."

I sighed. Did everything have to pass through me? I was only one person! "It's on my desk, Cynthia. You can't miss it."

What a nightmare! There was damage to the gym floor in addition to the doors, which were a total loss. The foundry that had made the statue had gone out of business five years ago, so good luck getting a replacement globe for Atlas. The district's insurance agent was on vacation for the next two weeks.

I missed my dinner meeting and my dinner. By the time I got back to my office, I was almost insane with aggravation. This was exactly why I couldn't tolerate screwups. There was no such thing as just one. The first led to the second, and pretty soon they were coming at you in battalions. I needed to accomplish one real thing on this miserable day, and I knew exactly what it was going to be: I was going to call that boy's parents and let them know the damage and chaos their son's vandalism had caused.

I scanned my desk for the paper where I'd written

his name. It was gone.

I scoured every item on that desk, and not just once. Nothing.

*"Cynthia!"*

But she had already left for the day.

How could this be? That boy must have snuck back in and stolen the paper, hoping I'd forget his name among the thirty thousand students I'm responsible for! Well, he was wrong about that! His name was—his name was—

Sudden overpowering chagrin.

I had broken my only rule.

# UNEXPLAINED
## DONOVAN CURTIS
## IQ: 112

f I didn't die of stress that night, I probably never will. Each time the phone rang, I was convinced it was Schultz, calling to rat me out to Mom and Dad. Every knock at the door meant the police were here to arrest the guy who'd bombed a basketball game with the weight of the world. Whenever my dad's BlackBerry pinged, I was positive that was the news-flash. It didn't make for good sleeping. It didn't make for *any* sleeping.

Mom was shocked at the sight of me over the breakfast table. "I was studying," I told her with a yawn wide enough to drive a truck through.

"You look like Wile E. Coyote after the Roadrunner dropped him off a cliff," said my sister, Katie. She was twenty-six, and had moved back in with us while her husband was deployed to Afghanistan with the Marines.

"Thanks, Miss Goodyear," I retorted absently. Katie was seven months pregnant, possibly with a baby hippo.

"One more wisecrack about my sumo stomach and I'll sit on you," she threatened. "You think this is a vacation for me?"

"Not for you; for *Brad*," I returned. "He's got an eleven-thousand-mile buffer zone from all this sweetness and light."

I regretted it the instant the words passed my lips. Normally, the two of us could go back and forth insulting each other for hours. But Katie lapsed into a melancholy silence, a far-off expression in her eyes. It wasn't hard to figure out the cause of her reverie. The father of her unborn child was on the opposite side of the world in a war zone. And even though First Lieutenant H. Bradley Patterson spent most of his time inside the armored shell of a tank, it had to be on her mind that her husband was in a risky line of work.

Mom came over and placed her hands reassuringly on Katie's shoulders. "Brad's surrounded by the best-trained people with the best equipment money can buy."

But her daughter's mind turned out to be elsewhere. "Beatrice is coming."

"Beatrice?" Mom echoed. "You mean Brad's dog? I thought she was staying with your mother-in-law."

"She *was*," Katie explained miserably. "But Fanny called me this morning. She said she can't cope, and she's coming this afternoon to drop off Beatrice."

"We're getting a dog?" I asked, mildly interested.

"That mutt hates me," Katie moaned. "That's the reason she was supposed to go to Fanny in the first place. Beatrice will never forgive me for taking her place in Brad's life. For all I know, she blames me for getting him shipped out. Like I make deployment decisions for the Marine Corps."

"She's your dog too, Katie," Mom lectured. "And we'd be delighted to take care of her while Brad's serving his country. Right, Donnie?"

"I'm not touching the poop scoop," I said firmly.

My mind was on Schultz, not dogs, that morning. At school, I waited to be called to the office. Between classes, I searched for the summons taped to my locker. Nothing. The anxiety was eating me up from the inside. When the PA announcement finally came, it was almost a relief.

"Would Donovan Curtis please come to the office? Donovan Curtis to the office."

It was the longest walk I'd ever taken. At each open door, hostile faces glowered out at me. Remember, I was still the guy who disrespected our beloved basketball team. When the news got around that I was also responsible for unleashing the runaway globe that bowled out the gym, I was really going to be Public Enemy Number One.

At last, I rounded the corner, and the glassed-in reception area came into view. To my surprise, the avenging angel waiting for me was not Dr. Schultz, but Mr. Fender.

"When you serve a detention with *me*, Mr. Curtis, you serve it to the end. And you don't leave until *I* tell you it's time. . . ."

He went on for a while, trying to scare me, I guess. The poor guy had no way of knowing that, considering the payback I was expecting from Schultz, a rampaging grizzly couldn't scare me. He cut me loose, though, explaining that, thanks to the damage to the gym, we students had "suffered enough."

I had a sneaking suspicion Schultz wasn't going to see it that way.

I couldn't say how much anybody had actually suffered, but the disaster at the basketball game was definitely the hot topic at school.

"When the glass blew out, I thought it was an explosion!"

"Like a terrorist attack!"

"Did you see the statue with the top part missing? It looks like my grandfather when his back goes out!"

"I heard the gym floor is permanently messed up!"

"When they catch the guy who did it, they're going to hang him on a meat hook!"

"Yeah!" Nussbaum chimed in. "I pity that poor loser! His life isn't worth a used Kleenex!" He turned to me. "So, Donovan, when do you think you're going to get busted?"

"Shhh!" I pulled the Daniels into the boys' room, and checked the stalls for possible eavesdroppers. "This is no joke! The walls have ears!"

"Dude." Nussbaum was offended. "We'd never rat out a friend."

"Listen, that call was a false alarm—just Fender for skipping out of detention. I don't understand why

Schultz hasn't come after me yet."

"Maybe he doesn't know who you are," Sanderson suggested.

I shook my head. "He wrote down my name. I told him where I go to school. He's the superintendent. He's got access to every file and record there is."

"Yeah, did you pick the wrong guy to get caught by or what?" Nussbaum agreed. "The head honcho of the whole district."

"I'm wondering if it's not as bad as it looked," I mused in a low voice. "A little cleanup, a little wood polish—"

"I heard they're going to have to redo the whole gym floor," Sanderson put in. "It costs, like, zillions of dollars."

"And don't forget the glass doors," Nussbaum added. "You're a dead man walking."

I totally agreed. So why wasn't it happening? All day long, and the following days too, I squirmed while rumors spread like head lice and the Daniels predicted my downfall. There was no escape from the tension at home, where reports of firefights in Afghanistan dominated CNN. Then, on Wednesday, Katie's mother-in-law dropped off the dog.

The times I'd seen Beatrice, she was a rocket-powered

hairball. But the cinnamon chow chow that slunk into our house was listless and mewling.

"What's wrong with her?" Mom asked.

"She's dying!" Fanny declared dramatically, and tried to walk out the door.

Katie held on to her arm. "How do you know? Did she get hit by a car? Is she sick?"

Her mother-in-law wasn't interested in the details. "I can't cope with this at my age!" And with that, she was gone.

Mom reached down to pat the dog. Beatrice snapped at her hand. She tossed a warning growl over her shoulder at Katie, just in case she might be contemplating a similar move.

"She's too mean to die," I observed.

"She can't die," Katie said tragically. "Brad loves her."

"Brad loves *you*, too," I returned. "What does that say about Brad?"

"He'll never forgive me if something happens to her!"

"Well, that's not exactly fair, is it?" Mom put in. "If anything went wrong, it was on Fanny's watch, not yours."

"That's her whole modus operandi," Katie argued.

"The minute she saw the writing on the wall, she dumped the dog on me! And how can we take care of Beatrice if she won't even let us go near her?"

As if in answer, Beatrice picked herself off the floor, walked over to me, and lay down on my feet.

"Donovan!" my mother exclaimed.

"What did I do? I didn't do anything!"

"Beatrice likes you!" Katie said in an awed whisper.

"So?"

"So you can look after her," Mom reasoned, like this was a huge honor.

I declined. "Forget it. Besides, if Brad is such a baby about Beatrice, you have to wonder if he's the right person to be in charge of a twenty-million-dollar tank."

But when Beatrice refused to eat, I had to hand-feed her a few lumps of liver-flavored kibble. When it was time to take her out, I was the only one she would allow to put the leash on. When Katie made her a bed in the basement, she wouldn't even go down the stairs. I knew I was going to have a roommate. Just call me Dog-Whisperer Donovan. As if I didn't have enough hassles.

Dad came home at six, bringing the mail. "There's a letter from the school, Donnie. Is there anything you want to tell us before we open it?"

By that time, my tongue was stuck to the roof of my mouth, so I just shook my head and waited for the ax to fall.

Who knew how much trouble I was in? Suspended? Probably. Expelled? Not out of the question—especially since Schultz thought I'd done it on purpose. I *had* done it on purpose—the hitting-the-statue part, anyway.

While Dad read, I monitored the telltale vein in the top left corner of his forehead. It bulged a little, but not nearly as much as it had during the aftermath of the toupee liftoff. That had to be considered an encouraging sign.

At last, he handed me the letter. "You have an explanation for this?"

"I—I—" Where would I even start?

My eyes fell on the page.

> *To the parents of DONOVAN CURTIS:*
> *The time has come to recognize your child's hard work*
> *and commitment to excellence as a student in the*
> *Hardcastle Independent School District. This letter is*
> *to inform you that DONOVAN has been selected to*
> *attend the Academy for Scholastic Distinction (ASD),*

*a special program geared toward gifted and talented
students, tailored to their exceptional abilities and
extraordinary potential for academic achievement. . . .*

It said more—a lot more, about school transfer paper-
work, and registration forms, and which bus route
would take me to my new placement at the Academy.
I barely saw any of it. My eyes couldn't get past words
like *excellence*, *distinction*, *gifted*, and especially *Donovan
Curtis*.

Gifted? *Me?* I was the guy who skateboarded down
waterslides and shot a Super Soaker at an electric fence.
When people heard my name, they thought, *Don't try
this at home!* not *gifted*.

I wasn't being expelled; I was being *promoted*.

Dad was grinning from ear to ear. "I always knew
that the real problem was they just weren't *challenging*
you."

Mom looked worried. "Is everything okay?"

"Donnie's gifted!" Dad crowed.

"It's a mistake," Katie scoffed. "The kid's about as
gifted as a caterpillar. He brings home a B and it sets
off six days of skywriting and fireworks."

Much as I hated to agree with Katie, she had a point.
My grades weren't terrible, but they were nothing to

write home about. Come to think of it, I *remembered* the day all the nerds and brainiacs took the special aptitude test to see who got into the gifted program. I remembered it because nobody even asked me to give it a try. And I wasn't insulted because I *wasn't gifted*.

My eyes skipped down to the bottom of the page.

*My heartiest congratulations once again. Your child is a credit to the Hardcastle Independent School District.*
*Sincerely,*
*Dr. Alonzo Schultz*
*Superintendent, HISD*

Schultz.

The only program Schultz would recommend *me* for was Alcatraz. Didn't he realize who I was? I mean, the guy made a point of getting my name so he'd know exactly who to burn at the stake!

It came to me in a giddy flashback to the day of The Incident. Right after Schultz let me go, his secretary asked for the roster of new kids for the Academy. The superintendent's response was the last thing I remember before bouncing out of there.

His exact words: "It's on my desk, Cynthia. You can't miss it."

Had that big doofus scribbled my name on the gifted list by accident? And everybody else thought it was there because it was supposed to be? It seemed crazy, but it did explain the two inexplicable things going on in my life right now: 1) why Schultz hadn't come to kill me yet, and 2) why I'd just been invited to go to genius school.

I laughed out loud. People thought *I* acted without thinking? This was a thousand times worse than hitting a statue with a twig. It was a shoo-in for the Bonehead Moves Hall of Fame!

"What's so funny?" Dad asked.

I almost spilled the beans. How many chances do you get to show that the guy who runs the entire city school system is an even bigger dipstick than you are? Besides, it's not like my parents weren't going to find out *eventually*. Sooner or later, Schultz would realize his mistake and . . .

Or would he? The only district officials who saw me that day were Schultz and his secretary, and neither of them had ever met me before. They worked in the administration building, not Hardcastle Middle School. The paper my name was written on was surely gone now, crumpled up in a wastebasket or fed through a paper shredder. The one thing the superintendent knew about me was the school I went to. That was the only way he could get to me.

The gifted letter tingled in my hands. If I was at the Academy, he wouldn't be able to find me. It was the realm of brainiacs and goody-goodies, the last place you'd look for a kid who put a bronze globe through a glass door.

A tiny voice spoke up from the depths of my spleen: *Forget it. Not in a million years. You won't last ten minutes in the gifted program. There's never been anybody more ungifted than you.*

Mom was flushed with happiness. "I always knew this day would come. It was only a matter of time before people realized how special you are." She sniffed back a tear of emotion. "Beatrice was our good-luck charm. Things are finally starting to turn around for this family. I can feel it."

"I feel it too," added Dad, putting his arms around her. "Wait a minute—*Beatrice?*" His eyes strayed to the hall, where the languid chow chow was chewing on his newspaper, reducing it to an inky pulp.

Up until that instant, I honestly don't think I was going to go through with it. But since Brad had shipped out and Katie had moved back in, the tension in our house had been simmering just below the boiling point. And now this extra stress with the stupid dog. How could I pile my own problems on top of that? Especially when Mom and Dad looked so proud—something that didn't happen every day where I was concerned.

I thought of my namesake, James Donovan, on the foundering *Titanic*. What would he do—sink or swim?

"Gifted," I said a little louder, as if trying it on for size. "I guess I'd better go to school and clean out my locker."

# UNARMED
## CHLOE GARFINKLE
## IQ: 159

*<<Hypothesis: Being gifted is not a gift.*
*A gift you get for nothing. This you have to pay for.>>*

Okay, I know it's not a *real* hypothesis—by that, I mean something you can design an experiment to test. But it's true. There's a *price* to being gifted.

The cost is your life. You don't die or anything like that. But you don't live either. Free time? Forget it. You go to a special academy that gives you extra work to suck up every spare minute—especially since it probably takes forever to get there. Schools for the gifted are few and far between. Chances are you don't live near one. Friends? Those are the people you slave alongside. They might be awesome, but how would you ever find out? You're too busy for them, and they're too busy for you. Sports? When? And besides, why play when you probably stink?

<<*Hypothesis: Athletic ability exists in inverse proportion to intelligence. Technically untrue—there are plenty of smart athletes. But not many compared with the number of brilliant sofa spuds.* >>

What about TV or video games? Oh, please. You're far too smart for that. Pep rallies? For what—the robotics team? Forget it—and the same goes for school dances, funny-hat day, drama club, charity drives. . . .

"Dances?" repeated Abigail Lee when I brought up the subject in homeroom. "Who do you want to dance with? Him?" She pointed at skinny, needle-nosed Noah Youkilis.

She had a point. Most of the guys at the Academy for Scholastic Distinction weren't exactly what you'd call Hollywood hunks. I didn't expect body-builders, but it would be nice if they could grow a set of shoulders between the lot of them. And it wouldn't hurt to spend a little time outdoors to put some color in those prison-pale faces.

<<*Hypothesis: Sunlamp-enhanced computer monitors, perhaps . . . ?*>>

Then again—being smart requires you to examine things from all sides—why pick on the guys? We girls weren't exactly homecoming queens either. Abigail was a genius biochemist, but her greatest fashion statement was her white lab coat. She looked like she hadn't combed her hair since 2007. Or me, for that matter. I'd scored a perfect 2400 on every SAT practice test since sixth grade, but who was I to talk? Here I was, almost fourteen, and I'd never danced with a guy who wasn't related to me. I'd never been to a party except for kiddy things with balloons. I wasn't going on the cover of *Seventeen* anytime soon, that was for sure.

"Okay, so it doesn't have to be a dance," I told Abigail. "But why can't it be *something*? Every day millions of kids around this country do millions of normal activities, and they have a great time at it. Why can't we?"

"The statewide robotics meet is coming up," she offered.

Sigh.

I took robotics. I was good at it. I was good at *all* of it. I totally belonged at this school. But why did it have to mean that I couldn't be a regular person too?

Mr. Osborne, our homeroom teacher, who was also head of the robotics program, breezed into the lab. "Let's hurry up and take attendance. We've got a lot to do today."

We were all there. Where else would we be? We were any teacher's dream, yet at that moment it made me sad. I had no desire to cut class—but maybe that was the problem. When was the last time one of us broke the rules? This morning, while checking on my experiment in the growth of hydroponic flax, I'd noticed the paper I'd taped to my desk lamp to concentrate the beam onto the seedlings. It was a certificate of merit I'd received for perfect attendance at school. I'd earned seven of these over the years, and what use were they to me? Makeshift lampshades.

<<*Hypothesis: Is there a point where the robotics student becomes the robot?*>>

When was the last time anybody even showed up late?

"Sorry I'm late." A tall sandy-haired boy appeared at the door. "Is this Mr. Osborne's class?"

"This is the robotics lab," the teacher replied. "And you are?"

"Donovan Curtis," the newcomer replied, waving a

printed form. "I'm supposed to be in this homeroom."

"Right—our fresh blood from Hardcastle Middle." Oz accepted the paper and examined it.

Abigail leaned over to me. "That can't be right! *He's* coming to this school?"

I was intrigued. "You know him?"

"We went to the same elementary. He's the kid who jumped off the roof with one of those Gymboree parachutes."

I sized him up. He was kind of cute in a careless, windblown way. Great eyes—black fringed, pale blue. "Well, he must be smart if he passed all the tests to get in here."

Abigail was unconvinced. "Maybe. But he would have had to change a lot since I knew him."

I bit my tongue. Okay, so Abigail thought he was dumb, but next to her, *everybody* was dumb. *I* was probably pretty dense compared with her. If Donovan Curtis didn't measure up to Lee standards, that hardly made him stupid. There were no dim bulbs at our school. But that's not to say that we didn't range from somewhat bright to superbright—and in a few cases, like Abigail and Noah, supernova.

She was telling me about Donovan getting his tongue frozen to a chain-link fence one winter, but by that time I'd stopped listening. I'd never met this new kid, but I already had him perfectly sized up in my mind.

Donovan Curtis was *normal*.

Normal! We had a lot of talents in our homeroom. Normalcy wasn't one of them. Noah's IQ was off the charts, but he'd yet to hold a conversation with a real human being this year. Most of the time, he didn't even make eye contact. He always seemed to be speaking to the empty space over your left shoulder. Or Jacey Halloran, who had already discovered an uncharted galaxy, but still couldn't figure out how to open a combination lock. Or Latrell Michaelson, our mechanical marvel, who took cars apart and put them together again blindfolded—for fun. He couldn't manage to wrap his mind around the fact that he had to wait in the food line to buy his lunch. Every single day was World War Three in the cafeteria.

We had kids who had set academic records, and published books, and won every conceivable prize and honor. We had kids who could quote you the exact line of dialogue that's spoken 94 minutes and 30 seconds into *The Matrix* or *Return of the Jedi*.

What was missing was somebody—*anybody*—normal.

"I am the great and powerful Oz," Mr. Osborne told the newcomer in a mystical tone—he said that to everybody the first time he met them. "Technically, this is homeroom 107, but you've probably noticed that it looks like a cross between a mad scientist's lair and a garbage dump. We do robotics here. Even if you're not taking robotics this semester, I hope you'll help out with the team. It's a pretty big deal here at the Academy." He turned to the rest of us. "Guys, meet Donovan. Donovan—the guys."

There was a very lukewarm chorus of greeting. Another thing about the Academy—being gifted rarely extended to social skills. My enthusiastic "Hi!" stood out embarrassingly over the murmurs.

Donovan ignored us. Instead, he faced our latest robot, a work in progress for this year's competition. "What's his name?"

We were all stunned.

Noah spoke up. "It's not a *he*; it's an *it*. It's a mechanical device, and, as such, has no name."

Donovan blinked. "Robots have names. Haven't you ever seen *Star Wars*?"

Was he kidding? Half of us could recite *Star Wars*.

"We've been doing this for a long time," Abigail informed him in a superior tone. "We've made the finals three years in a row, and we did it with science, not by calling our entry Harry or Fred."

A few others spoke up in agreement. To be honest, I was on their side. The robot wasn't a toy or pet; it was a machine. I kept my mouth shut, though. Poor Donovan had only been in our class about thirty seconds, and we were already jumping all over him.

It didn't seem to bother the newcomer. "Okay, no name." He turned back to the robot. "Sorry, Tin Man." Oz on the brain, I guess.

He grabbed hold of one of the forks of the lifting assembly and gave it a hearty handshake. With a snap, it came off in his hand.

There was nothing lukewarm about the class reaction to that. A babble of outraged accusations filled the lab. Abigail, our team captain, was on her feet barking, "You broke it!"

Donovan tried to press the broken fork back onto the chain drive. It clattered to the floor.

"All right! Quiet, everybody!" Oz held his arms up for order. "Donovan didn't break anything. The component hadn't been attached properly." He turned to his newest student. "But it's not a bad lesson for your first day in the lab."

"I won't mess with any more of your—stuff,"

Donovan promised, chastened.

The robotics teacher shook his head. "I *want* you to mess with stuff. This is a place of tinkering, fiddling, experimentation. But," he added pointedly, "before you touch, *ask* somebody."

"Especially before you touch Tin Man," Latrell added feelingly.

"He's a delicate piece of equipment," Abigail pointed out. "And he's *not* Tin Man."

I was fascinated. Now everybody was referring to this array of nuts and bolts and circuits as *he*. Was it possible that in *not* naming our robot, Donovan had just named our robot?

<<*Hypothesis: A name changes an "it" to a "he."*>>

Kevin Amari raised his hand. "Even though he's not Tin Man, is it okay if we call him Tin Man for short? 'The robot' is so impersonal."

"Maybe because he's *not a person!*" By this time, Abigail was gritting through clenched teeth.

"He's not actually made of tin," Noah mused thoughtfully. "But I guess Aluminum Man isn't appropriate either, since he's also made of titanium, steel, plastic, various polymers, and silicon computer chips."

"How about Metallica?" suggested Latrell.

"That's good too," Donovan approved. "Anything

but 'the robot.' Poor guy."

"Squarepants," Kevin offered. "You know, because he's so boxy."

"Oh, perfect," Abigail snarled. "Now all our hard work is named after a cartoon!"

"Let's live with it for a while," Oz put in hurriedly. "We don't have to decide right away."

Amazing—in a few minutes we had gone from no name to three. And all because Donovan Curtis had walked into our school.

I kept an eye on him through homeroom. Except for the mishap with Tin Man—or whatever the name was going to be—I saw no sign of the buffoon Abigail had described. If anything, Donovan was trying to be friendly—not that he was getting very far with our crew. Engaging Noah in conversation isn't the easiest thing to do under the best of circumstances. But Donovan was asking him for advice on what to expect in some of his classes.

"Well," Noah replied thoughtfully, "math is easy, and the only thing easier than chemistry is biology or maybe physics. Social studies—easy. And English— well, you get the picture."

Poor Donovan just stared at him. He'd probably

spent his entire life hearing stories about the Academy's killer courses and crushing workload. And here Noah had dismissed them all in the space of about eight seconds.

<<*Hypothesis: If you want a realistic assessment of a challenge, don't ask the guy with the two hundred IQ.*>>

If Donovan had inquired about unraveling the genetic code, Noah would have said that was easy too.

"Thanks, I guess," Donovan told him. "Is anything in this place—well—hard?"

"You know what's hard?" Suddenly, Noah's face flushed with emotion. "Trying to control your own destiny. It's not just hard; it's impossible."

So Donovan shifted gears and talked to Latrell about the robot, which also backfired. Latrell got weirdly defensive, as if Donovan might be trying to steal his job as the team's top mechanic. And Jacey became so genuinely flustered by the newcomer's presence that she asked him which of the earth's continental plates was his favorite.

Abigail went over to Donovan and put her two cents in. "You know a Gymboree parachute isn't the same as a real parachute, don't you?"

Well, how could I *not* say something? He was going

to think we were all nuts.

I caught up with him in the hall on the way to first period. "Hi, I'm Chloe Garfinkle from homeroom."

I held out my hand, and he shook it lightly. Maybe he expected it to break off like that piece of robot.

"Hey, don't worry about the lift mechanism," I soothed. "The weakness probably came from a bad weld that got jarred loose by the chain drive, or maybe too much compression from the Bimba cylinder."

He looked blank. "What's it for?"

"Oh, the Bimba cylinder provides the pneumatic pressure—"

"I mean Tin Man," he corrected. "What does he do?"

"The robot has multiple capabilities," I enthused. "The electric eye can navigate color-coded tracks on the floor. The forks pick up inflatable rings that the lift mechanism places on various pegs at different heights. And it—uh—*he* can deploy a mini-bot that will climb a pole and strike a bell at the top."

He seemed confused. "Is that how geniuses spend their time? Picking up toys and ringing bells?"

I bristled. "You're here, aren't you? If being smart's such a crime, you're just as guilty as the rest of us!" He had no answer for that, so I went on in a calmer tone, "Noah's the only one who's *really* a genius. Except that the work is a little more challenging, how's the Academy any different from Hardcastle?"

He gave me a half smile. "Seriously?"

"If there's one thing we're good at here," I assured him, "it's being serious."

"Have you ever been to Hardcastle Middle School?" he asked.

"I know we probably take some things for granted—"

"But they're probably not the things you think. If you want to plug in a computer, can you find an outlet with three prongs? Can you find one that even works? Will part of the suspended ceiling come down on your head in the middle of class? Will the cafeteria refrigerators break, so you can't buy lunch for a day, or a week, or a month?"

"Hey, things like that happen at the Academy too," I insisted, almost triumphantly. "Last year the freezers failed so there was no ice for"—the wind went out of my sails as I realized how lame this was going to sound—"the sushi bar."

He nodded sympathetically. "You guys should get T-shirts made. You know: I Survived the Sushi Crisis."

"Hey!"

"All I'm saying is that you brainiacs have a nice racket going here."

I skewered him on that point. "Don't you mean *we* brainiacs? You're one of us now."

"Right," he agreed, flustered. "But—well, I just got here, so you've been riding the gravy train longer."

"Regular school has its advantages, right?" I didn't want to seem dorky, but I was genuinely interested. "Dances, parties . . ."

A shrug.

"Pep rallies, sports—the basketball team is all-city. Wasn't there some kind of huge accident at their last game?"

His eyes narrowed. "What do you know about that?"

"Everybody's talking about it. A piece broke off this statue. . . ." My voice trailed off. Why did he seem so suspicious? I was only trying to be friendly, and he was acting like this was a CIA interrogation under hot lights.

"I don't go to that school anymore," he said very sharply, almost like he was mad at me. "I'm too— smart." And he stormed away, leaving me standing in the hall with my mouth hanging open.

It wasn't his rudeness that struck me. It was this: Ever since I'd started at the Academy, the one thing I'd been yearning for was somebody normal. Now, finally, he was here.

<<*Hypothesis: What if the normal people are even weirder than we are?*>>

# UNKNOWING
## DONOVAN CURTIS
## IQ: 112

**W**hen the paper airplane bounced off the back of the driver's head, the man pulled the bus over onto the shoulder. He got out of his seat, picked up the offending aircraft, and waved it at us.

Honest—it wasn't me. The last thing I wanted to do at the Academy was draw attention to myself. But I was so used to getting blamed for stuff that I braced myself for the onslaught.

"Interesting experiment," the driver said in an

approving tone. "The air moves with the bus, so the plane flies normally. An open window would interfere with that. The more open windows, the greater the interference. And if the bus had no roof, the plane would be half a mile behind us."

Whoa, even the Academy bus drivers were gifted! If you chuck a paper airplane at someone, they assume you did it for science. On my old bus, the driver would have held us all hostage until we gave up the person who did it—probably me. And you can bet that "interesting experiment" wouldn't have been what he called it. *Mutiny*, maybe. Or *armed insurrection*.

There was a smattering of applause as a seventh grader, flushed with triumph, reclaimed his plane, and we were under way again.

Soon we arrived at the Academy for Scholastic Distinction, which looked absolutely nothing like a school if you ask me. It was, by far, the most modern building in town. Every inch of the place was covered with solar panels. On sunny days, it was like pulling up to a jewel-encrusted palace. Supposedly, the students had worked with the architects who designed it. The Academy was 100 percent eco-friendly, right down to the bathrooms, where the toilets had different "flush settings," depending on the kind of waste you were getting rid of. There was no button for "cherry bomb," which is what the teachers invested a lot of energy preparing for at my old school.

Mr. Del Rio, the principal, stood outside the automatic sliding doors greeting his students with handshakes. At Hardcastle Middle, you never saw the principal unless you did something wrong—which, in my case, was fairly often. Mom always used to say, "Donnie gets a lot of personal attention at the very highest level at that school." She was so proud that I was at the Academy now. I felt a pang of guilt for the bogus reason behind it.

Determination surged through me. Maybe I could hack it here. After all, half of being gifted was just the fact that everybody *expected* you to be smart. Like that seventh grader on the bus. No way was that any experiment. The guy made a paper airplane, and he couldn't resist flying it. Well, Couldn't Resist was practically my middle name. I wasn't that different from the Academy kids. Obviously, I was never going to star at this place. But with hard work, a little bit of luck, and a lot of good acting, I might just be able to fake it.

*If* x *represents the vector of variables,* b *and* c *are vectors of known coefficients, and* A *is a matrix of* *coefficients, determine the maximum value of the objective function $c^T x$ . . .*

I stared at the problem until my liquefied eyeballs were about to drip out of their sockets and roll down my cheeks.

All around the math room, my classmates were working away, calculating and figuring. It went without saying that I couldn't *do* it. Man, I couldn't even *read* it.

In the next row, Noah Youkilis was scribbling away like it was the easiest thing in the world. The kid really *was* gifted—although anybody who looked like Noah and *wasn't* gifted would have a genuine complaint. Picture a four-foot-eleven praying mantis suffering from extreme malnutrition, with a long nose and glasses that were last in style when President Truman wore them.

As he plowed methodically through the page, I couldn't help noticing what a dark pencil he was using. The numbers really stood out against the bright white of the worksheet. Another thing about me— I've been blessed with excellent peripheral vision. Well, what was I supposed to do—sit there while the period ticked away? According to ancestry.com, my great-great-great uncle was a "spotter" during World War One—he floated over the battlefield in a hot-air balloon and peered down into the German trenches. It didn't explain much about me, since he never tried to bungee-jump out of the basket. But it was probably why it was so easy for me to copy the answers off Noah's paper.

I tried to get a few wrong, which was actually pretty tricky. I understood so little that it was impossible to know what a reasonable mistake might be. Even cheating was harder in this place.

Noah scrambled up on scrawny legs and handed his paper to Ms. Bevelaqua. "I'm done."

She glanced at it and then handed it back without so much as notation. "All right, Noah. Do it properly this time."

The praying mantis hunched a little farther forward. "I'm working to the best of my ability! It's not my fault this math is too hard! I'll never get it right!" His lower lip quivered.

The teacher nodded understandingly. "Poor you. It isn't easy to master calculus in middle school."

"This isn't calculus; it's linear programming!" Noah blurted. "Everybody knows that!"

"Right," she said triumphantly. "Including you."

She motioned him back toward his seat.

He looked bummed at getting caught, but he couldn't have been half as bummed as I was. In a class of geniuses, I had copied from the guy who got it wrong on purpose.

Luckily, there were plenty of fish in the sea. I leaned a little closer to Abigail Lee, who was motoring through the assignment at almost-Noah speed. I remembered her from elementary school, where she'd been all-universe at anything that took brains. Her writing wasn't quite as clear, but beggars can't be choosers. At least I had the reasonable belief she wasn't trying to fail. What was up with this Noah kid, I couldn't imagine.

"Hey!" Abigail hunched over, blocking my view of her paper. "What do you think you're doing?"

I played dumb. "What?" I covered my worksheet, like I was preventing *her* from copying from *me*.

*"Ms. Bevelaqua!"* she bawled. *"Donovan's cheating!"*

"Chill out," I tried to hiss.

"I'm not going to chill out! If we have the same answers we'll both get zero! I've never had a zero in my life! I can't get zero! I work too hard to get zero! What am I going to tell my tutors if I get zero?" She was red in the face, heading for purple.

Noah seemed genuinely bewildered. "Well, if you're

looking for the *right* answers," he asked me, "why don't you just *calculate* them?"

"Big talk from the freak who goes out of his way to put down the wrong ones!" I retorted.

That got Chloe's back up. "Watch who you're calling a freak, you—*troglodyte*!"

"Yeah?" I spat back. "Well, I don't know what that is, so trog-whatever to you too!"

Then this girl Jacey, who said random things at moments of stress, announced, "In Brazil more cars run on ethanol than regular gas."

It had the effect of a referee's whistle, separating the combatants from their clinch.

I learned a few things in that class. First, the regular student code about not ratting people out—that didn't apply at the Academy. Second, nobody knew how to deal with cheating, because it never happened. No one needed to do it. Third, *zero* is a four-letter word.

Amazingly, I didn't really get in trouble, although it was pretty obvious who was copying from whom. I wasn't sent to the office; there was no detention; nobody even yelled at me, which was a first in my educational experience. Instead, my homeroom teacher, Mr. Osborne, came and suggested we take a walk. At Hardcastle Middle, if you're caught off campus during school hours, they've practically got guard towers to gun you down. I was beginning to see that they had two sets of rules in our district—one for the brainiacs, and one for everybody else. Of course, I was living the good life now. But I still took it personally since I knew it was all a mistake.

"Look, Donovan," Mr. Osborne said pleasantly, "at the Academy, we've got kids who are talented at a lot of different subjects. But very few of us are good at *everything*. If you're not up to this math, it's no disgrace to admit it. In fact, it happens all the time. We have regular classes too."

I nodded dumbly.

"This is a period of discovery," he went on. "We're getting to know you, and you're getting to know us. And during that process, we'll explore where your true gifts lie. Are there any fields of study that really turn you on?"

I hesitated. Sooner or later, somebody was going to realize that my presence here was completely bogus. But—also sooner or later—my namesake, James Donovan, would have joined his fellow *Titanic* passengers on the bottom of the ocean. He'd survived by staying afloat until the rescuers could get to him—*by making it later rather than sooner!*

I had to keep swimming.

"I think," I said aloud, "that we should stick with the exploring part a little while longer."

He nodded approvingly. "Very wise. Let's not rush into anything. But promise me you'll join the robotics team and help out with Tin Man. I mean—our entry."

"Last time I touched Tin Man, his hand fell off," I reminded him gently.

He shrugged it off. "You'll watch and learn. That's what the Academy is all about."

"Thanks, Mr. Osborne," I mumbled.

"Call me Oz."

I hate it when adults do that.

The Hardcastle Mall used to be one of my favorite hangouts. Tonight, though, it looked a little drab and in need of a face-lift. It wasn't the mall that had changed. It was just that school was newer, nicer, and cleaner. The Academy, not Hardcastle Middle, obviously. Our cafeteria had better options than the food court, and the prices were lower.

We didn't even have the dumb rules that ruined everything. For example, soda was banned at my old school because of the sugar content. But the Academy lunchroom had a drink machine that was open to everybody. It even sold the extra-sugar, extra-caffeine stuff. It was fine, even necessary to fuel the brainiacs through late-night studying marathons. But if one of the ungifted kids at Hardcastle happened to get a sip, he'd go straight out and rob a bank.

Technically, my six-month ban for swimming in the fountain was still in effect. But the security guard who had busted me wasn't on duty. It was a bum rap. It isn't skinny-dipping if you're wearing boxers. Besides, if the air-conditioning is going to break down on a ninety-degree day, it's management's responsibility to fix it before people start looking for other ways to cool off.

The Daniels had never experienced the Academy cafeteria, so they thought the food court was fine dining. We weren't eating anyway. I was on a bench, trying to ignore the Daniels' whooping and yipping, designed to catch the attention of a couple of girls.

"Do something funny, Donovan," Nussbaum urged. "Chicks eat that stuff up."

I glared at him. "If you want to talk to Heather Mahoney, why don't you walk over there?"

"Because that would be lame," he explained reasonably. "*She* has to come to *me*."

"Jump in the fountain again," Sanderson urged me.

"That's an attention grabber."

"*You* jump in the fountain," I shot back.

He grabbed me under the arms, but I disarmed him with a punch to the gut before Nussbaum could help him wrestle me into the water.

It did the trick, though. Heather and her friend—Deirdre Somebody—were ambling in our direction.

"Hi, Donovan," Heather addressed me. "Haven't seen you for a few days. Were you sick?"

"Donovan's a genius now," Sanderson supplied. "He goes to the gifted Academy."

"Really?" Deirdre was impressed. "Don't you have to take a lot of tests for that?"

"It's no big deal," I put in quickly, studying the floor.

"You're telling me!" Nussbaum exclaimed. "You know how he got picked? He's only there because—"

I stomped on his sneaker hard, silencing him before he could say more.

"Donovan!" came another voice.

It took me a second to recognize her. It was Chloe from the Academy. She said something to a middle-aged woman and headed toward our table.

"Who's that?" Sanderson asked.

"She's in my new homeroom," I replied.

Nussbaum snickered. "Nice lumberjack shirt."

Funny—surrounded by the kids at the Academy, Chloe looked kind of good. Call it the Youkilis factor; the gifted crew wasn't exactly Fashion Week. Yet next to Heather and Deirdre, you could tell she was out of her league. Those two wore skinny jeans and vintage T-shirts that were just—well, *right*. Chloe wasn't ugly or anything like that—in fact, she had a pretty face. But you had to concentrate to notice it. She wore no makeup, and her loose flannel shirt gave her a lumpy appearance. A huge button on her lapel declared: THAT'S OKAY, PLUTO. I'M NOT A PLANET EITHER. It clanked as she walked.

I was surprised to see her at all outside of school. I always thought of her as one of those people who suddenly whooshes into being at the sound of the first bell in the morning, and winks out again when the clock strikes three-thirty.

"Hi, Donovan," she greeted me eagerly. "Do you live around here?"

"Hey, Chloe." She was looking expectantly at the others, so I semi-introduced them. "Meet the guys."

"Hi, Chloe." Nussbaum stepped forward and pumped her hand. The grin on his face was barely this side of idiotic. "How does it feel to have Donovan in the Academy? I mean, is he gifted or what?"

"I think it's 'or what,'" Sanderson said with a smirk.

Chloe could tell they were messing with her, but she had no idea how much. "Donovan's cool," she offered tentatively. She turned back to me. "Sorry about what happened in math today. How did it go with Oz?"

For some reason, I felt I had to defend myself. "I never meant to cheat off Abigail. I was *trying* to cheat off Noah. How was I supposed to know he puts down the wrong answers on purpose? I thought he was this big genius."

"He definitely doesn't feel the need to prove it," she replied with a sympathetic smile. "Abigail's the opposite. If she ever brought home a B-plus, it would be the end of the world."

"She practically tore my head off."

"She's under a lot of pressure," Chloe explained. "She does just about everything, and she's keeping half the tutors in town in business. She pushes herself pretty hard."

"I never thought the gifted kids had problems," mused Deirdre.

"It's those big brains," Nussbaum supplied wisely. "It makes a person top-heavy, out of balance. Like the Atlas statue."

"How crazy was that?" Heather exclaimed. "I was at

the game! The girl at the end of my row was covered in broken glass!"

"They still haven't found the guy who did it," Deirdre added.

"I heard it was an accident," I suggested, looking daggers at Nussbaum. "Wear and tear on the statue. It can't be easy to hold up the weight of the world in the wind and rain year after year—especially when it's attached by one bolt."

"One bolt," Chloe repeated dubiously. "That's pretty shoddy engineering. We put more thought into Tin Man's stress points."

"Tin Man?" Sanderson echoed.

"Our class robot," I answered, and bit my tongue. "I mean the robot that happens to live in the homeroom I got assigned to."

"It's your robot, too," Chloe said generously. "You're on the robotics team now. Maybe you'll put us over the top at the big meet. We've come in second to Cold Spring Harbor three years in a row."

You could just see the Daniels swelling up with joy at this new information. Not only did I go to the nerd school, but I was on the robotics team, which was nerd squared. No way could I ever live this down in only one lifetime.

Chloe waved at the woman she'd arrived with. "Got to go. My mom's done shopping." She beamed at me. "See you tomorrow."

"See you," I mumbled.

"We should hop too," Heather put in. "Our ride will be here any minute."

I hated to see them leave. When it was just me and the Daniels, I knew I was going to get it.

Nussbaum didn't disappoint. "Some girlfriend you've got there, Donovan. Or is she just a regular friend, and you're dating Tin Man?"

"I can't believe Tin Man's cheating on Tin Woman." Sanderson clucked disapprovingly. "She must be hot. She probably doesn't wear her grandfather's plaid shirt."

"Shut up, you guys. Chloe's not my girlfriend and it isn't my robot. I'm only on the robotics team because my homeroom teacher is the coach. I have to try to fit in over there, and believe me, it isn't easy—and not just because I haven't got the brainpower. You heard about the guy who tried to flunk the math test—the teacher had to trick him into admitting he understood it. So he's a genius and a moron all in one. It's a nut-house!"

"Well, it's not safe to come back to Hardcastle yet,"

Sanderson advised. "We had an assembly today, and that guy Schultz was standing right at the door. He looked at every single face that came into the gym. I'll bet he's searching for you, man! He didn't even stick around. He just watched us file in and took off."

I felt ice-cold tentacles wrapping around my stomach. It was my worst fear coming true, but at least it settled one issue. All day I'd been asking myself what I was doing at the Academy for Scholastic Distinction. Now I knew.

I was hiding out.

# UNCREDITED

## MR. OSBORNE
## IQ: 132

f I didn't know better, I'd swear that Donovan Curtis wasn't gifted at all. I'd bet a month's pay that an eighth-grade boy had been chosen at absolute random and dropped into the top academy for differentiated instruction in the state.

But I did know better. Our selection procedure was ironclad. Students had to pass a battery of tests from the state department of education, not to mention faculty interviews, and even a psychological exam. A mosquito couldn't make it through the screening process.

Our last faculty meeting was essentially a seminar on Donovan Curtis. It turned out to be quite a revelation. All his teachers had realized that he was weak in their courses, and had assumed that his gifts lay elsewhere. But after comparing notes, it became clear that his gifts lay *nowhere*. He was mediocre in English, social studies, French, and computer science, and well below average in math and science. I didn't expect him to excel at *everything*, but Donovan excelled at *nothing*. Which begged the question: What was he doing at the Academy?

"Have you tried getting him involved with the robotics team?" asked our principal, Brian Del Rio.

I nodded. "He's our designated Googler."

"Your what?"

"He has no knowledge of programming, engineering, hydraulics, pneumatics, or even basic mechanics. So he surfs the internet looking for pictures to download and paste on Tin Man. Like Albert Einstein eating a banana."

Brian frowned. "What's Tin Man?"

"The robot. It's short for Tin Man Metallica Squarepants. Donovan's idea."

"You don't think he's putting us on, do you?"

suggested Ellie Shapiro, the department head for social studies. "Some of these bright kids have a warped sense of humor."

"I doubt it," I told her. "To be honest, the other kids love what he does with the graphics. And nobody's ever thought of naming the robot before. I admit I wasn't too crazy about the idea. At first I only went along with it to empower Donovan. But you know what? I'm glad we did it."

"It's very cute," Ellie agreed.

"It's more than cute," I amended. "It's humanized our entire program. The difference between dealing with an *it* and a *him* is a transformative concept."

"Maybe that's our answer," Brian mused. "Dozens of brilliant kids pass through your class, building machines that win prizes at the highest levels. Yet the simplest thing—naming a piece of equipment, or decorating it—gets by everybody except Donovan."

Maria Bevelaqua—math—spoke up. "Or he does it because he can't do anything else. He doodles through my class. He hasn't taken a single note."

I jumped on this. "A photographic memory?"

"He's lucky he can remember his own name," she deadpanned. "I asked him what school he came from, and you know what he said? 'I forget.' If that's a photographic memory, he left the lens cap on."

"Perhaps it's a kind of social intelligence," Brian ventured, really reaching.

"Oh, please," Maria snorted. "He may seem like a smooth operator compared to our usual clientele. But there's nothing special about him in that way either."

"I have to agree," I said wearily. "He alienated Abigail on day one. And he causes a lot of friction in the lab. Latrell feels threatened by him, and Jacey doesn't know what to make of him."

"Jacey doesn't know quite what to make of anyone," Ellie cut in.

"Chloe comes the closest to understanding him, but they butt heads too," I went on. "And as for Noah—"

"Noah's so smart that most of us can't even begin to imagine what's going on in his head," Maria put in.

I sighed. "Maybe. But the reverse is also true. Noah can't understand not understanding. And there's Donovan, who understands *nothing*. To Noah, he's like some exotic space alien who crash-landed in the gifted program."

"Maybe Noah isn't wrong about that," Maria challenged.

Brian's brow furrowed. "What are you saying?"

"What if," Maria went on, "our much-vaunted

selection system broke down and sent us your average knuckle-dragger?"

"Impossible." Our principal was adamant. "All our kids have strengths and weaknesses. We seem to have a good sense of Donovan's weaknesses. It's a start. Now we have to find his strengths. He wouldn't be here if they didn't exist."

As the meeting broke up, he pulled me aside. "There's one more thing." He hesitated. "You're not going to like it."

I sighed. "Let me guess—Donovan again?"

"This time it isn't Donovan. As you may know, all students graduating from middle school are required to complete one quarter of Human Growth and Development."

"Human Growth and Development?" I echoed. "You mean sex education?"

He made a face. "We haven't called it that in decades."

"But what does that have to do with me?" I asked. "They teach that in seventh grade, don't they?"

"Usually . . ." The principal took a deep breath. "Your kids don't have it."

I was horrified. "None of them?"

"None of the big names—Youkilis, Halloran, Garfinkle, Lee. A few transfers took the equivalent at their old schools. And Donovan's okay—he got the instruction at Hardcastle."

"How could we miss that?"

Brian shrugged unhappily. "Robotics has always attracted our best and brightest. Anything new and innovative and exciting is thrown at your group. They're always busy. And the last thing anyone thought they needed was to spend hours drawing diagrams of the human body and watching videos on how babies are made."

"So what happens now?" I asked wearily. "I have to drop what I'm doing, and spend the rest of the year on . . . sex ed?"

He shook his head. "You need a state certification to teach Human Growth and Development. You're not qualified."

"So who is?"

"Nobody," Brian told me. "Beth Vogel has been coming over from Salem to work with our seventh grade, but she's teaching a full schedule this quarter. The whole district is running on austerity. Staffing is cut to the bone. Believe me, Oz, I've been over this every which way with Dr. Schultz. If there were a way out, we would have found it. The state allows us absolutely zero flexibility. Forty hours under a credentialed teacher, with triple time credited for real hands-on experience."

"They're kids, Brian! Where are they going to get hands-on experience of *that*? Would we even want them to?"

"We're still working on a few possibilities," he admitted. "They could take the course after school. Or over the summer."

"Think of the students you're talking about," I pleaded. "They take music lessons, learn languages, intern at research labs, work with private tutors. They're scheduled down to the nanosecond. You're going to make them give up all that for *sex ed*?"

"Human Growth and Development," he amended.

"We ought to be ashamed of ourselves!"

He nodded grimly. "We are."

I was heartsick. "What am I going to tell the kids?"

"Don't tell them anything yet. Not till we've explored every option."

Privately, I was hoping that one of my colleagues might bail me out on the Mission Impossible of Donovan and his hidden talents. Every time another teacher approached me, I expected the eureka moment—"I've got it! He's a brilliant . . ." I didn't care what came next—writer, physicist, harpsichord player, linguist, chess master, infrared astronomer; he has total recall, perfect pitch, a knack for languages, great potential for spelunking. Anything!

It was a cop-out. The answer wasn't going to drop from the sky and land at my feet. I'd watched him in my own classroom. Why would he be different anywhere else?

Actually, he did *less* for me than he did for the other teachers. At least in his core subjects, he tried and failed. In robotics, all he did was search the internet for graphics to stick on Tin Man. Seriously, to justify the time he spent on Google Images, we would have needed a robot the size of a twenty-story building.

A convulsive high-pitched cackling filled the lab. When I went to investigate, I found Donovan at the keyboard and Noah peering over his shoulder—holding on to it, in fact—hysterical with laughter.

Noah *never* laughed. He had a stratospheric IQ with few commonsense skills, and zero sense of humor. His thinking was lightning fast and flawlessly accurate, but also 100 percent literal. I barely recognized him, convulsed with mirth, breathing hard, his face bright pink.

"What is it?"

"Look—" He pointed at the screen, bereft of speech.

On the screen, a brief video clip showed a barefoot man walking along the edge of a pool. He stubbed his toe on a rubber dog bone and tumbled, arms flailing, into the water. Noah pounded on the desk, choking.

Chloe appeared at my elbow. "It's called YouTube, Noah."

"It's the latest thing," Donovan added. "Ten years ago."

"*That's* YouTube?" Noah was incredulous. "I've heard of it, obviously, but I never—who's the actor? He's brilliant! I really *believed* that he fell in the pool by accident."

I sighed. Of course a kid like Noah had never explored YouTube before. When he got on a computer, most of us couldn't imagine what he was capable of. What he *wasn't* capable of were the ordinary things.

"He's not an actor," I explained patiently, "he's a regular person. Anyone can post a home video on YouTube."

He was wide-eyed. "Anyone?"

"And anyone can watch it," Donovan confirmed.

Noah may have started the day a YouTube novice, but by the end of the period, he could have written a doctoral dissertation on it. Such was the power of his intellect. He took Donovan's seat at the computer, and disappeared into the site, reappearing only occasionally to explain the math behind his estimate of the total number of videos—over eight hundred million—or the amount of time it would take to watch them all—more than six hundred years.

"Assuming an average duration of twenty to twenty-five seconds each," he concluded. "I'll be more precise when I've had a few weeks to study it."

"Way to go," Abigail told Donovan savagely. "Noah should be curing diseases and changing the world, not watching some dimwit falling in his pool."

"Give the guy a break from his brain," Donovan argued. "When's the last time anybody saw him so psyched about something?"

I had to give Donovan that. For all Noah's incredible abilities, the boy would fail out of school if his teachers were to let him. Donovan alone had managed to engage him. Could that be a kind of giftedness in and of itself?

Regardless, Donovan had succeeded in running through yet another class without yielding the slightest hint as to why he was at the Academy.

Of all the kids in my homeroom, Chloe was the one most taken with Donovan. It was a crush, not so much on Donovan himself as what he represented—normal middle school life. She peppered him with questions about parties and school spirit and big games and pep rallies.

"I wasn't really into that stuff," Donovan told her.

He was reluctant to talk about his experiences at Hardcastle Middle. Something must have gone on there that I couldn't quite put my finger on. He seemed anxious to put the past behind him—anxious enough to ignore the obvious signs that he wasn't fitting in here. Had he been bullied? A lot of our students had suffered that at their old schools. But Donovan didn't seem like the type.

Chloe would not be put off. "Well, there must have been parties," she reasoned. "You know, dances—that kind of thing."

"I think it's a pathetic waste of time," Abigail chimed in. "Can you imagine having nothing better to do than bounce around a school gym to bad music under cheap streamers and a cheesy rented disco ball? Don't we all have better things to do?"

"No argument from me," said Donovan.

Nothing pleased Abigail less than being agreed with by Donovan.

"Hey, you guys—do something funny," Noah waved

at us from behind a flip video camera. "This is for YouTube."

The kids ignored him, but I felt it was important to support Noah's new interest. For all his brilliance, Noah spent his life in a kind of cocoon. Pointing a flip cam at people was as close as he got to social interaction.

"What about Tin Man?" I suggested. "He looks like a YouTube star to me."

Abigail was horrified. "That's a terrible idea! We'd be showing the other teams exactly what we're working on for the robotics meet!"

I chuckled. "It's supposed to be a friendly competition, Abigail, not a life-and-death struggle."

Never try to tell Abigail to take it easy.

"The results of that meet go on your permanent record," she insisted. "There could be college admissions on the line, maybe even scholarships. If that's not a life-and-death struggle, I don't know what is! This could be the year we finally defeat Cold Spring Harbor and win it all! Do you want to risk that?"

Eventually, we shouted her down. If Cold Spring Harbor found our little clip among six hundred years of video on YouTube, they *deserved* to beat us again. And anyway, some of the kids were already rolling

Tin Man Metallica Squarepants out into the middle of the room.

I had to admit, our latest creation was taking shape. No credit to me—everything had come from the kids. Abigail and Chloe provided the design, and Noah did all the programming. The boy had never watched YouTube, but he could think in computer code. Kevin was our welding and soldering expert. Jacey and Latrell built the body. And there, large as life on Tin Man's "chest," was Albert Einstein eating a banana, courtesy of Donovan. There were other graphics too—a cat with a Mohawk, the fiery eye of Sauron from the *Lord of the Rings* movies, the flag of Mozambique, and a bumper sticker that read OFFICE OF NEW YORK CITY RATCATCHER.

Noah brandished the flip cam, and Abigail worked the joystick, sending our work in progress on its first trial run. The robot was capable of moving on its own, following a route marked by colored lines on the floor. But the most important rounds of the competition required a human driver.

I watched carefully, taking special note of the wheels, which were a new type for us. Last year, Cold Spring Harbor had used Mecanum wheels, which gave them extra maneuverability. But on Tin

Man, I couldn't see much difference.

"Hold it." I got down on all fours and examined the bearings to make sure the Mecanums had a full range of motion.

"The problem's not the wheels," put in Donovan. "It's the driver."

Abigail glared at him. "What do you know about robotics?"

"Nothing," he replied honestly. "But I can use a joystick. Don't you guys play video games?"

"I'd like to see *you* do better!"

And with a casual shrug, he held out his hands for the controller. Eyes shooting sparks, Abigail relinquished it, and Donovan put Tin Man through his paces. I watched in amazement. The robot fairly danced around the lab, the lift mechanism moving easily. The Mecanums worked like magic, changing direction instantly with a flick of Donovan's wrist.

The kids broke into cheers. They mobbed Donovan, begging him to be our operator at the meet—all except Abigail. She stood rooted to the floor, fuming.

"Got it!" Noah lowered the camera and ran for the computer to upload his very first YouTube video.

And me? Well, I was thrilled for the team and tantalized at the prospect of finally giving Cold Spring

Harbor a run for their money. But I also realized that my chief problem was no closer to a solution. Being good with a joystick because of hundreds of hours playing video games was not the kind of talent that got a student into the Academy for Academic Distinction.

What was Donovan Curtis doing in the gifted program?

# UNREPAIRED

## DONOVAN CURTIS
## IQ: 112

The grade glowered at me off the cover sheet of my social studies paper: D-minus.

"Is that graded on a bell curve?" I asked Mrs. Shapiro.

She was almost sympathetic. "No, Donovan. It's just graded."

"Oh."

I wasn't normally grade-obsessed, but this really threw me. The thing is, I had no chance with the kind of math and science they taught in this place. If I was going to have any prayer at all of hacking it in the Academy, I'd have to rock subjects like English and social studies. That's why I was so shocked about the D-minus. I'd worked really hard on this paper. Maybe I hadn't aced it by gifted standards. But I'd figured I'd get a least a B. I would have settled for a C!

The teacher sighed. "Is there anything you want to tell me? Is something wrong?"

Something was wrong, all right. When the biggest effort I'd put into a school project since kindergarten pulled a D-minus, yes, it was pretty fair to say that something was wrong.

She interpreted my silence as an invitation to probe further. "At home, perhaps?"

"Well, it's just that I have ADD." That was pure blind inspiration. Sanderson had ADD, and occasionally he got cut a little extra slack because of it.

Mrs. Shapiro's expression softened immediately. "Why didn't you say so?"

"I guess I was too distracted by other things." She looked a little suspicious, so I added, "I really wanted to make it on my own. ADD doesn't sound very gifted."

"That's nonsense," she reassured me. "You'd be

astounded how often giftedness is accompanied by some sort of learning disability." She handed the paper back to me. "Why don't you work on this for another week?"

I didn't like the sound of that. "Well . . ."

"And we'll see what we can do about raising your grade."

Hmmm, maybe there was more to this learning disability racket than met the eye. After all, ADD was just the beginning. With a little bit of effort, I could work up a case of obsessive-compulsive disorder that would knock your socks off. And what about dyslexia? That could be just the ticket to ward off any D-minuses that might be coming down the pike in English.

I put my all into the social studies paper, and Mrs. Shapiro grudgingly upped me to a C. I fared no better in English class. Dyslexia or not, C-minus was the best I could come up with, and that was a stretch. Have you ever read *Beowulf*? Even the Cliff Notes could kill you.

I expanded my list of disorders. Restless leg syndrome was a good one. It explained all my fidgeting. And my nonspecific bladder issues allowed me to spend as much time in the bathroom as outside of it. I had this recurring nightmare that all my teachers got together and compared notes on my various illnesses, weaknesses, and diseases. At the end of the dream, an ambulance pulls up to the Academy to haul me off to intensive care. But when the attendant takes off his surgical mask, it isn't a paramedic; it's Dr. Schultz. Then I'd wake up, choking and spitting, because Beatrice was sleeping on my face.

Yes, the chow chow was still a fact of life—I should say a fact of *my* life, since she totally loved me. Props to Katie—she tried to help out. But every time she even got in the same room with her husband's dog, Beatrice growled her off. All the mutt wanted was me. She spent her nights in my bed and her days in my dresser drawer, because my scent was on my sheets and clothing—which meant I spent nights *and* days scratching at itchy dog hair. There wasn't a part of my body the chow chow hadn't napped on yet. I should open up for business as a parking lot. I'd make a fortune in dog biscuits.

I would have put a stop to it, except that I was beginning to think Brad's mother was right. Beatrice really *was* sick. Her energy level was absolute zero, and she ate nothing at all, which was amazing, because her stomach seemed fatter than ever. Nussbaum's pet snake had more get-up-and-go. When the cold-blooded animals are livelier than the warm-blooded ones, you know you've got a problem.

Katie was freaking out. "If anything happens to Beatrice, Brad's going to drive his M1 halfway around the world and run me over."

"Not a good idea," I told her. "You're a pretty big speed bump. We don't want to owe the Marines a new tank."

Poor Katie: her belly was expanding, her butt was widening, her ankles were thickening, and her varicose veins looked more like a road map every day. She was almost as big a mess as Beatrice—except that Katie hadn't started peeing on the floor.

That unpleasant surprise came in the form of a warm puddle on the carpet as I made my way downstairs for breakfast.

"That mutt has got to go!" I howled, hopping on the steps, pulling off my soggy sock.

My dad grinned at me from the front hall. "Is that how you support our troops? By evicting their pets?"

"I don't want to live in a chow chow's toilet!" I complained.

He laughed appreciatively. "Good thing you went to charm school before you got picked for the Academy." Even Dad cut me a little slack these days. No wonder the gifted kids were different. They lived in a bubble. "I'm going to pick up a carpet steamer on my way to work this morning. Change your socks. I'll give you a ride."

Outside, my eyes were drawn to the new bumper sticker on Dad's car:

PROUD PARENT OF AN HONOR STUDENT

AT THE ACADEMY FOR SCHOLASTIC DISTINCTION

"I'm not an honor student," I managed, understatement of the year. "I just go there."

He was unperturbed. "Everybody's an honor student at that place. It's an honor just to walk in the door. We're all proud of you, Donnie. Your mother and me, Katie—"

"Right," I snorted. "She said I'm dumber than her bladder-challenged dog."

Dad started the car. "She may not say it in so many words, but don't think she isn't feeling it. These are tough times for our family, what with Brad deployed and the baby coming. And now Beatrice—like we don't have enough stress in our lives already. Then you step in and do something for everybody to feel good about. It's like it was sent from heaven."

I felt as if I was losing my mind. Hiding out in the gifted program, and carrying the emotional well-being of my entire family. No pressure.

At the small appliance shop, I hung back while Dad spoke with the salesman. There was a copy of the town paper lying open on the cashier's desk. I nearly threw up my breakfast when I read the banner headline:

REPAIRS IN LIMBO THANKS TO "STATUE-GATE"

*Physical Education classes at Hardcastle Middle and High Schools are being held outdoors despite the frigid winter temperatures. The glass double doors of the athletic facility are still boarded shut, and 25 percent of the floor is badly damaged. The school district is ready to roll on the repairs; a contractor has been hired.*

*So what's the holdup?*

*The Parthenon Insurance Group is refusing to pay, arguing that the damage was caused by "engineering negligence" in the statue of Atlas, a portion of which rolled down the hill and smashed into the building. The offending object, Atlas's "globe of the world and heavens"—all 400 pounds of it—was affixed by a single bolt, which corroded over the years. This "design flaw,"*

*Parthenon argues, is the responsibility of the statue's manufacturer. However, Classical Bronze Foundries, Inc., went bankrupt in 1998, leaving the school high and dry.*

*The Hardcastle School District has filed suit against Parthenon, but the case is likely to drag on for years, according to Superintendent Alonzo Schultz. In the meantime, the physical education program is out in the cold. All varsity basketball home games have to be relocated, and even the middle school's annual Valentine Dance will take place elsewhere. Dr. Schultz holds out little hope for an early resolution unless he can track down a "person of interest" in the case. . . .*

Yikes! If the insurance company stiffed the school district, would this "person of interest" have to pick up the tab? It wasn't my fault Schultz cheaped out and bought a bum statue from a company that went bankrupt! Classical Bronze Foundries probably tried to save a few bucks on bolts and had to pay it all back a hundred times over in lawsuits.

But I'll bet our superintendent was the only genius who put *his* Atlas at the top of a hill overlooking a breakable gym!

With a sinking heart, I watched Dad haggling with

the salesman, trying to save every penny. We weren't poor, but money was tight, especially with an extra mouth to feed—Katie—and a baby on the way. The one good thing about Beatrice's hunger strike was that we weren't blowing a fortune on dog food. There was no way we could afford to fix a busted gym. It didn't take Noah Youkilis or Abigail Lee to do *that* math.

I got to the Academy earlier than usual, which gave me some much-needed extra time to work on my science project. Abigail's was entitled "The Abiotic Synthesis of Organic Compounds"; Chloe's had something to do with the wave/particle duality of light, whatever that is; Noah's, "The Youkilis Constant," was this number he'd developed that supposedly explained the expansion of the universe in the first few seconds following the Big Bang. Mine was called "Chow Chows: A Special Breed." Obviously, it wasn't as impressive as the others, but I was really slaving over it. My plan was this: I was never going to outscience the Academy kids, but I could give it the personal touch. Hey, if I was stuck being hospice nurse to a dying dog, at least I should get a project out of it. I had photographs, and sound recordings of barking, and microscope slides of fur and drool samples. If I loaded up enough stuff, Mr. Holman would have to give me a decent grade on sheer volume. And if he turned out to be a dog lover, I'd be golden.

I stashed my coat in my locker, which was still basically empty. Lockers were huge at the Academy. I'd never seen it, but supposedly one kid kept a full tropical fish tank in his, plugged into the built-in power strip. Unlike Hardcastle Middle with its no-phones-during-school-hours rule, the Academy encouraged its gifted students to have laptops and smartphones charged up and available at all times. "You never know when the research bug might hit," Mr. Osborne was fond of saying. It made me smile that Noah—apex of the IQ pyramid—now used his BlackBerry purely for watching YouTube.

The robotics lab was deserted when I got there. "Hey, Tin Man," I said, greeting him in a low voice, bestowing a very gentle high-five on one of the lifting forks.

Call me crazy, but it sort of pleased me that the robot had a name thanks to me. Just like it pleased me that I was now Tin Man's first-string driver for the robotics meet. I know that must seem pretty stupid coming from someone who was in such big trouble in every other phase of his life.

Standing there next to Tin Man, I happened to glance over to the teacher's cluttered desk. There was an internal memo form on top of the mess. My eyes froze on the subject line: "SUMMER SCHOOL."

It had to be about me. Who else in this class of brainiacs could possibly need summer school? In the interest of self-preservation, I had to read it.

*Oz—as we feared, the district has been unable to find a certified teacher to offer Human Growth and Development to your students who have unfortunately missed it. Summer school appears to be their only option. The kids affected are Chloe Garfinkle, Abigail Lee, Noah Youkilis . . .*

That was as far as I got before Mr. Osborne came in and caught me snooping.

"Donovan—step away from my desk!"

I was too blown away to worry about whether or not he was mad. "Summer school!" I exclaimed. "For *those* guys?"

"It's none of your business," the teacher interrupted sharply. "It doesn't affect you at all."

"But why would the smartest kids in town need

summer school?" I persisted, bewildered. "What's Human Growth and Development?"

"It's a health course required by the state," he explained wearily. "You took it last year in seventh grade."

Light dawned. "And you were so busy teaching them genius stuff that you missed it." I mulled it over. "That's on you, not them."

He looked like I'd slapped him. "I know."

I would have bet money that I had absolutely nothing in common with my gifted classmates. But here they were just like me, getting jerked around because the school district had messed up. I was on the hook for the damage caused by Schultz's defective statue; they were on the hook for a required course nobody remembered they needed. And the cost was going to be one summer.

"So teach it to them," I concluded. "Those guys, it won't take ten minutes before they know it better than you."

He shook his head gravely. "The teacher has to be state certified. Or it has to come from hands-on experience."

"Hands-on experience?" I repeated, startled. "They want that? Isn't it all about—well, you know?"

"Physiology," he interjected. "Adolescence, body changes . . ."

The seed of an idea began to germinate in my mind. "What else?" I prompted.

"Reproduction."

Katie folded her arms atop her big belly. "You're out of your mind," she told me. "I always knew you were crazy, but this is proof positive."

"Don't be like that," I wheedled. "It won't cost you anything except a few trips to the school. Why should you care? You'll be pregnant anyway."

"It won't cost me anything?" she echoed. "How about my privacy? My dignity? My self-respect? My right to bring a baby into this world without turning it into a science fair project?"

"It isn't even for me," I argued. "These kids really need your help. They're in a jam."

She was adamant. "Well, if they're so gifted, let them find a way out of the jam."

"You have to do this for me," I said stubbornly.

"No way, Donnie. Not in a million years. I'm not crawling into a petri dish for you or anybody."

I sighed. "Well, okay. I feel sorry for Brad, though."

She was wary. "What's Brad got to do with it?"

"You know, there he is, far from home, serving his country. It'll break his heart when he finds out his beloved dog isn't getting the care and attention she deserves." I pointed to Beatrice, who was making another liquid deposit on the rug.

She shrieked so loud that it brought Mom running up the stairs. "What's wrong?"

"Nothing, Mom," I called. "But fire up the carpet steamer, will you? We're going to need it in a few minutes."

Katie was beside herself. "Just what are you saying?"

"Do I have to spell it out for you? If I don't look after Beatrice, Beatrice doesn't get looked after."

"And that's my fault?" she demanded. "She won't let me anywhere near her."

"I totally sympathize," I assured her. "Bad things happen to good people sometimes. Look at the poor Academy kids. It isn't their fault they missed this credit, but they're the ones who have to suffer. Just like it isn't your fault your mother-in-law dumped a dying dog on your doorstep."

"Don't say 'dying'! She's not dying! She can't—" Suddenly, Katie clued in. "You miserable blackmailing slime bucket! This is low even for you."

I nodded in agreement. "Poor Brad."

She was bitter. "What do you care if a bunch of nerds go to summer school? You already took this course. There's nothing in it for you!"

She was only half right. There *was* nothing in it for me—at least nothing I could explain to Katie. If this worked—if following Katie's pregnancy could count as hands-on experience for Human Growth and Development—that would strengthen my ties to the Academy for Scholastic Distinction. It wouldn't make my grades any better, but it might take people's attention off how ungifted I was. The longer I could stay at the Academy, the longer I could keep myself hidden from Schultz's justice.

Selfish? Big-time. And something else, too: It was absolutely what James Donovan would have done. Maybe ancestry.com wasn't such a waste of money after all. The Hardcastle gym may have been my *Titanic,* but we were survivors, James and me.

Aloud, I said, "I'm doing it because a nice person helps his friends."

She rolled her eyes, but I knew I had her.

# UNSURPRISED

## CHLOE GARFINKLE
## IQ: 159

<<*Hypothesis: Donovan Curtis is smarter than
all of us put together.*>>

Okay, probably not. Make that definitely not. Yet all our spectacular grades, killer IQs, and gang-buster test scores couldn't keep us out of summer school. Neither could Oz, Mr. Del Rio, and even Dr. Schultz. And Donovan managed it with a flick of the wrist.

The stomach entered the room first. It was enormous,

like someone had stretched a tablecloth over a prize-winning watermelon. We waited for the rest of her to come in. It took longer than we thought because she wasn't moving too swiftly. When I finally saw how petite she was, it seemed like a miracle she was moving at all.

Her name was Katie Patterson, and she was Donovan's older sister. This was kind of like Show and Tell on steroids. She was our Human Growth and Development project, our way out of summer school. We needed final approval from the state, of course. But Oz and the school agreed that she counted as hands-on experience, provided we followed her pregnancy for its final six weeks.

I'd known the minute Donovan showed up in the lab that something important was happening. And here was the proof. He was the cavalry, galloping to our rescue. Can you imagine the top students in the state, and maybe even the whole country, not being allowed to start high school? It would be a huge black eye for the Academy and the whole school district. And what did Donovan get out of this? Nothing. He'd already taken Human Growth and Development, so *he* wouldn't have to go to summer school. And he had a sister who didn't exactly look thrilled that he had volunteered her unborn child as our class pet. So he was probably going to pay for it at home.

Abigail said Donovan was a self-centered jerk, not gifted at all, who was laughing at us behind our backs. I didn't agree. Maybe he wasn't gifted in the way we were, but he had an uncanny knack for making a difference. Take the robotics program. From a scientific standpoint, Tin Man hadn't changed at all since his arrival. Donovan had contributed a name, a few pictures from the internet, and his joystick skills. Yet somehow he'd transformed our entire team. We were focused, excited, united. Cold Spring Harbor had better watch out.

<<*Hypothesis: The whole is greater than the sum of its parts. Especially if one of those parts is Donovan.*>>

"Welcome to the robotics lab, Katie," Oz greeted the newcomer warmly. "We're so grateful to you for helping us out by allowing us into your life."

She glared in her brother's direction, then turned to the teacher. "I have only one rule, and this one's a deal breaker. When you're seven and a half months pregnant, you go to the bathroom every time the wind blows. So when I have to run, nobody had better get in my way."

Oz seized the teachable moment. "What happens is

the growing baby expands the uterus, and puts pressure on the bladder."

"Whatever the reason," Katie continued, "when I've got to go, everything else is on hold. I don't care if I'm performing CPR and have to leave one of you gasping and suffocating. Are we clear?"

<<*Hypothesis: The Belly Rule—whoever has the belly makes the rules.*>>

"First off," Katie told us, "being pregnant is the weirdest thing that's ever going to happen to you. It's like growing a whole extra body part that doesn't seem to do anything except bump into furniture, and slowly get bigger so you can bump into even more furniture."

I raised my hand. "But aren't you excited?"

"I was," she admitted. "But then six months go by, and you stop believing that it's ever going to happen. It's hard to maintain the fever pitch for almost a year." Her expression grew sad. "And it's hard to think that, when this baby is born, its dad won't be there to see it."

"When did he die?" came Noah's nasal voice.

Donovan brayed a laugh right into his face. "He's not dead, wise guy! He's a tank commander in Afghanistan, and he won't be home in time!"

Oz jumped in. "You get used to Noah," he said quickly. "He's not being insensitive, I assure you."

Katie nodded. "Another thing about being pregnant—your body, which used to be your own private business, is suddenly a hands-on theme park for total strangers. Everybody in a white coat pokes, prods, or examines you in some way or another. And for what they can't see, they have plenty of sophisticated machines that can look inside you. I brought a few of my sonogram pictures if anyone's interested in having a look."

We all were. I think Katie was kind of surprised about that. She was used to Donovan and, let's face it, he was pretty different from the average gifted kid. None of us knew anything about pregnancy, or sonograms, but it was natural for us to take everything seriously and to do our best with it. We wanted to know about this because we wanted to know about everything. We were just knowers.

I scoured the black-and-white images, searching for anything that resembled a baby. I think I spotted a set of ribs, and maybe a foot, but I also saw something that looked like a bust of Abraham Lincoln, and that definitely wasn't in there. Abigail thought she'd found the head, but Katie explained that it was just a bubble in the amniotic fluid. Latrell was convinced he saw twins. Kevin and Jacey saw nothing at all.

Donavan wouldn't even try. "I'll have plenty of time to look at it after it's born. It's going to be my niece. Or nephew. Whatever."

Noah stepped forward for a closer look. "If it's a girl," he said finally, "then what's *that*?" And we could all see exactly what he was pointing at.

Katie looked both startled and forlorn at the same time. "We didn't want to know the sex. We wanted it to be a surprise."

"He could be wrong," Oz managed without much conviction.

The rest of us nodded in agreement, but we knew better. Noah was never wrong unless he wanted to be.

"Better start knitting blue bootees," Donovan told his sister.

She looked daggers at her brother. "Wipe that grin off your face, Donnie. I wouldn't even be here if it wasn't for you. So everything that happens is your fault!"

<<*Hypothesis: Brothers and sisters forge family bonds through a complex byplay of accusations and insults.*>>

It wasn't all business. Katie wanted to see the robot, so we gave her a little demonstration. And while Donovan was operating Tin Man, I ended up next to his sister.

"What's he like at home?" I whispered.

"He's a barrel of laughs," she replied. "He drinks orange juice out of the bottle, carpets his room in old socks, watches poker on TV, and has never said the words *thank you* in living memory. Should I go on?"

I felt my face flushing as I stuck up for him. "He's doing an amazing thing bringing you here for our class." She cast me a piercing look that instantly had me on the defensive. "What?"

"Nothing, really." She smiled at me. "It's just— interesting to see your brother through someone else's eyes."

And suddenly, just as Tin Man was deploying the mini-bot, she became very still, her expression far away.

"Are you okay?" I whispered in concern.

"The baby's kicking." She took my hand and placed it on the sweater over her rounded abdomen.

I could feel it tapping against my hand, like little hiccups. It was strange, but also kind of beautiful. I was so much more than just one hour closer to my

Human Growth and Development credit. In those sixty minutes, I'd learned what a brand-new human life felt like.

<<*Hypothesis: And a certain tank commander in Afghanistan will soon find out he's having a son.*>>

# UNFAILING

## NOAH YOUKILIS
## IQ: 206

These were my math test results for the semester so far: 0 out of 20, 1 out of 15, 4 out of 35, and incomplete.

This was my math grade on my progress report: A-plus.

I explained to Ms. Bevelaqua that my score was actually 4.52 percent, a solid F-minus on any reasonable scale. She just laughed, and changed the A-plus to A-plus-plus. Then she wrote in the "comments" section: "Computes averages without aid of calculator."

How unfair was that?

I found a clip on YouTube called "Failing Math." But when I watched it, it was completely unhelpful. They didn't teach you how to fail math; they taught you how to pass! I expected more from YouTube, which usually had great stuff, like wrestling videos, oranges that talk, and people putting out oil-well fires.

There was another video called "Failing Schools," but it turned out just to be this news story about how our education system isn't any good. I could have told them that. And not for the reasons *they* gave. The problem with our education system is if you score one little 206 on one little IQ test, everybody goes nuts about it. You have to go to a special school, only they call it an "Academy," which really just means the same thing. And then the pressure starts: Do better, reach for the stars, live up to your potential, go all out, strive, achieve.

Why?

"You've been blessed with an incredible gift, and you're wasting it!" Oz was constantly telling me. "You should be getting a hundred percent on everything!"

He wanted me to admit that I got 4 out of 35 on

purpose; that I could have gotten 35 out of 35 without breaking a sweat. That was missing the point entirely. To me this stuff was all so easy that 4 out of 35 and 35 out of 35 were really the same thing. It was like kicking puffballs of dandelion seeds as you walk across an open field. You *could* get them all. But why would you? It just didn't *matter*.

Abigail thought I was crazy. I disagreed. And if I was as smart as the IQ test said I was, which one of us was right?

I never asked to be right about everything. It just happened that way. When you have the answers before anybody asks the questions, nothing is very surprising, whether you're in the gifted program or not. You might as well go to the regular school around the corner from your house.

I wanted that *so much*. The students who went to that school laughed a lot. And even when they weren't in the act of laughing, they seemed *unpressured*. I could hear it in snippets of conversation as I waited for my bus to the Academy: "I don't care . . . who cares . . . I couldn't care less . . . ask me if I care . . . like I care . . ."

Everybody said they were less intelligent than us, but I thought those kids were really on to something.

At the Academy, people cared *too much*, which was why we laughed so *little*. And *unpressured* was the last word you'd use to describe us.

So why couldn't I convince my parents to let me transfer? Was that argument beyond even my intellect? Did it require an IQ of 207 or better? I was failing at failing. The teachers were on to me. They'd never let it happen.

There was a conundrum here:

*A) Only sheer genius could get me out of the Academy.*
*B) Anyone showing sheer genius is sent to the Academy.*

I used to spend many hours pondering this, back in the days when I had many hours to spend pondering. That all changed when Donovan Curtis told me about YouTube. This was an important revelation for me, because almost everything on YouTube is surprising. I'll never forget when Donovan showed me how to use it. He clicked on a video and, for eleven magical seconds, we watched a cocker spaniel drinking out of a toilet. In those eleven seconds, my world was transformed. What I had just seen could not have been predicted by anyone, regardless of IQ. It was astonishingly simple and utterly random—the brain hiccup of a collective mind seven billion people strong.

I'd been looking for something like this my whole life. And I was infinitely grateful to Donovan for opening that door for me. I almost forgave him for bringing in his sister and spoiling the only chance I might ever have to flunk.

The word had just come in from the state department of education that studying Katie Patterson's pregnancy officially counted as real-life experience in Human Growth and Development. You should have seen the celebration when Oz made the announcement in the robotics lab. Everyone mobbed Donovan, slapping him on the back and cheering. All except Abigail. She actually wept at the news that she wouldn't have to go to summer school. It was a little confusing. She took classes all summer anyway, so wasn't that summer school too? What was the difference between the summer school she went to on purpose and the summer school she'd do anything to avoid?

Speaking of confusing, there was Donovan himself. He clearly didn't belong at the Academy. I knew that after his first twenty minutes in the lab. What was he doing here? I had no idea—and that alone was considerably awesome. There were very few things that I had no idea about. The fact that one of them had landed a few seats away from me in homeroom was wonderful in itself.

Donovan was like a human YouTube video—unpredictable. We could have worked on Tin Man for years, incorporating every refinement allowed by technology. But none of us could have envisioned that the greatest improvement of all would be simply in the way you drove it. Yet when Donovan took over the joystick, the answer was right there for all of us to see.

It also made excellent YouTube footage. Google *Tin Man Metallica Squarepants Exposes Teacher's Underwear* and the clip should come up. It already had more than a thousand page views, making it my greatest hit so far. Picture this: Ms. Bevelaqua was covering for Oz in the lab, and one fork of the robot's lift mechanism got under her skirt. By the time she noticed it, her hem was up around her ears, and everybody was staring at her underpants, which were bright yellow with a pattern of Cartesian geometry.

Ms. Bevelaqua didn't accept Donovan's apology. You'd think a math teacher who wore Cartesian geometry underwear would have a better sense of humor. But she was really mad. Her face looked like she was being tasered—or at least how those people look in YouTube videos.

We were just getting calmed down after that brouhaha when Chloe pounded into the lab, gasping from an all-out sprint. "You won't believe it!" she panted. "They still haven't fixed the Hardcastle gym, so they're moving the Valentine Dance *here*!"

Donovan looked uncomfortable. "What do we care about another school's party?"

"Don't you get it?" Chloe crowed. "It's on our turf, so we're all invited! I've been in the gifted program since I was eight, and you know how many dances we've had? Try zero!"

"Except for 'The Dance of the Electrons,'" I reminded her. "My sixth-grade science project."

Abigail did not share Chloe's enthusiasm. "I can't think of a single thing that interests me less than a school dance."

Chloe stared at her. "But you're *going*, right?"

"Not even at gunpoint."

Chloe was devastated. "But you have to! We may never get the chance to go to another one!"

Abigail was adamant. "That suits me just fine."

"You're a scientist," Ms. Bevelaqua challenged her. "How can you arrive at a conclusion without any data to back it up?"

Chloe jumped on the bandwagon. "Look at this as

an experiment. A *social* experiment. Right, Donovan?"

Donovan shrugged. "Don't ask me. I never go to dances."

"Well, you're going to this one," announced Oz, striding into the room. "I'm making it a class assignment."

Abigail was horrified. "Oz—you can't make us go to an after-school event!"

"No," the teacher agreed, "but I can assign everybody to write an essay about it. And if you haven't been there, you'll have to take a zero."

"*I'll* take a zero," I volunteered readily.

"You couldn't get a zero if you handed in a blank page," Abigail said in a resentful tone.

She was tight-lipped, but I had a feeling she'd be there. I'd kill for a bad grade; she'd kill to avoid one.

Oz panned the room, making eye contact with each student. "This is a good idea, people. We're all so focused on our specialties that we tend to miss out on ordinary experiences. Having fun is part of an education too, you know."

"I don't have time to go to a dance," I complained. "In the three hours it would take me to get there, be there, and get home, I could watch between seventy and one hundred YouTube videos—depending on the duration of each, of course."

"There's more to life than YouTube, Noah," chided Chloe.

"That's where you're wrong," I retorted. "YouTube *is* life, only better. The entirety of human experience is on that little screen. Last night, I watched a modern-day clash of gladiators in bathing suits battling in and out of a roped square, jumping off tables and hitting each other with chairs!"

"It's called professional wrestling, Noah," Donovan announced. "And it's all fake."

"I saw blood!" I respected Donovan, but he didn't know everything. "If my mother hadn't pulled the plug on my computer, I could have watched a steel-cage match!"

Oz put an end to the discussion. "It's settled. We'll all be there. And there's extra credit in it for anybody who can relax enough to have a good time."

"Will you be going?" I asked Donovan as we headed back to our seats.

"I never went to Hardcastle dances when I was a Hardcastle student," he told me. "Why should I start now?"

Oz overheard us. "Extra credit, Donovan," he said

enticingly, dangling the prospect like a fisherman dangles bait.

"So you'll be there?" I persisted.

"What do you care?" Donovan snapped, suddenly angry. "*You* shouldn't even be going. You don't need extra credit. You've got more points than you know what to do with."

"I wish I could give you some of mine," I told him honestly. "But I don't think it works that way."

He stared at me for a moment, and then sighed. "See you at the dance."

# UNPASTEURIZED

## DONOVAN CURTIS
## IQ: 112

"**D**onnie!"

I was getting ready for school when the blood-curdling scream brought me running out of the bathroom.

*"Donnie, get in here this minute!"*

I leaped over Beatrice, who was sprawled across my doorway, and ran into Katie's room, preparing to dial 911. But she was alive and well, sitting at her laptop computer, reading her overnight emails from Afghanistan.

I reddened. "It was probably Noah. YouTube is his whole life."

"I'm entitled to a life too, you know!" she stormed at me. "That didn't change because you blackmailed me into signing on with your freaky brain trust! I found that video! It's basically a two-minute close-up of my fat belly while 'We Are the Champions' plays in the background!"

"It's a compliment. He's got nothing better to do with his two hundred IQ."

"Cut it out, Donnie. You're not talking to your misfits here—"

"They're not misfits," I insisted. "They're just—different. Supersmart. But dumb in a way, too. Like babies."

It was the wrong word. It reminded her. "My husband is eleven thousand miles away in a dangerous war zone. He shouldn't be hearing about his wife's pregnancy from YouTube. And his captain shouldn't be hearing about it at all."

"I'll get Noah to take the video down," I promised. "He didn't mean anything. You don't understand about him."

She looked curious. "What happened to you, Donnie? You're giving your best friends the cold shoulder, but defending these crazies?"

"I'm not—" I protested.

But she had a point. I *had* been avoiding the Daniels, who were being totally unreasonable about "sharing *our* Valentine Dance with a dweeb army." Sanderson's words, not mine.

"Poor you," I'd told him at the time. "If you're so offended by smart people, don't go."

"Deirdre's going to be there," he'd shot back. "And Heather. She's into you, man."

At that point Nussbaum had punched him in the gut. "Heather's into *me*!"

"Nobody's going to be into anyone when the Academy dorks suck all the coolness out of the air," Sanderson had complained.

That conversation really bugged me. I mean, nobody knew better than me that the gifted kids weren't exactly über-happening. But this was a school dance, not some A-list Hollywood red-carpet event. Like there weren't any uncool people at Hardcastle!

I faced Katie. "They're not crazy—most of them. Don't knock them. These days, they're your biggest fans."

She cast a sour look at Beatrice. "They're not exactly facing stiff competition in that department."

"Show some respect for the almost dead."

"That's not funny," she snarled through gritted teeth. "Did it ever occur to you that my marriage could be on the line over that dog? No, because it's all the same to you so long as your weird classmates get to paw the Incredible Expanding Stomach!"

I sighed. "If they're smart enough to predict supernovas on the opposite side of the galaxy, credit them with the brains to appreciate how you came to their rescue."

Her eyes narrowed. "There's something fishy about this whole gifted thing. It doesn't add up. I'm not saying you're stupid, but you're hardly the type to sniff around for extra work."

"I *didn't* sniff around. The Academy found me, remember?"

"I do remember," she conceded. "That's the fishy part. Anyway, we should get going. My appointment with Dr. Manolo is at nine-thirty."

I was attending Katie's next obstetric checkup—not as her brother, but as a member of Human Growth and Development 101. Mr. Osborne had gotten permission for a field trip, so our whole class was going. I hoped Dr. Manolo had invested in a spacious office.

Driving with Katie was an adventure these days. Her stomach was so huge that she had to set the seat all the way back. Her arms were barely long enough to reach the wheel, and she hunched forward, looking like Jeff Gordon wedged behind a giant beach ball.

We were just waddling in from the parking lot when the minibus arrived. You could tell they didn't get a lot of school buses at the clinic. In obstetrics, the only kids involved were the ones being born. And not too many pregnant women arrived with an entourage of brainiacs.

The doctor was running late, so we had to wait forty minutes, which wasn't exactly pleasant. Noah speed-read through two years' worth of *Mother-to-Be Magazine*, peppering Katie with questions like "Have you eaten any unpasteurized cheeses lately?"

"No," she grumbled. "Have you?"

"What's your opinion of giving the baby solid food before four months?"

"You're bringing back my morning sickness," she warned.

"Really? According to the June 2011 issue, that happens in the first trimester."

She glared at him. "It came back when they saw my stomach on YouTube—in Afghanistan."

Oz quickly stepped between them. "Let's give Katie a little space, Noah. This is *her* doctor's appointment, after all. We're just privileged to be here."

When we finally got called, the nurse said, "I'm sorry. Only immediate family in the examining room."

"They *are* family," Katie informed her with a sigh. "You know how you can't pick your relatives?"

The woman was adamant. "I'm afraid it's a privacy issue."

"I have no privacy," Katie replied wearily. "My stomach is on YouTube."

Oz was ready to back everybody off, but Dr. Manolo was kind of psyched to have an audience. He used to work at a teaching hospital, he explained. He missed having students around.

We kept our distance for the exam, of course, but we watched the sonogram, and we were all invited to put on the stethoscope and listen to the baby's heartbeat.

"Sounds kind of freaky," commented Latrell. "You know, listening to another person who's trapped in there."

Katie made a face. "I can't tell you how thrilled I am that my family planning is contributing to your horror-movie fantasy."

"It's a miracle," Chloe breathed.

Even Abigail's serious expression softened when she had the stethoscope on.

Oz assumed a far-off, dreamy expression. "I remember these appointments from when my wife and I were expecting our own kids. There's nothing quite like it."

The doctor kept Katie a few minutes extra. When she stepped out into the waiting room, the students of Human Growth and Development 101 leaped to their feet and gave her a rousing standing ovation. Their enthusiasm was so infectious that everybody in the reception room joined in—all the other expectant moms and dads and family members.

Katie was so taken aback that she actually did a little curtsy, blushing deep mauve. "I didn't do anything," she insisted. But the smile on her face was 100 percent genuine.

Katie headed home alone, and I got on the minibus

with everybody else for the ride to the Academy.

"How was the field trip?" asked the driver. "Fun?"

Chloe nodded enthusiastically. "We were at a pelvic exam!"

"And we listened to a fetus," added Noah.

The driver seemed bewildered.

"We're gifted," I explained.

# UNSUCCESSFUL

## DR. SCHULTZ
## IQ: 127

**W**ell, my "no screwups" rule was pretty much out the window. My life had become one big screwup after another.

Three weeks had now passed, and not a single repair had been made to the Hardcastle gym. Frankly, no one was doing anything about anything. The insurance company was digging in its corporate heels, and we had no option but to dig in ours. The instrument of destruction, Atlas's detached "globe," was collecting dust in the basement of the administration building, next to old filing cabinets and a lawn tractor that was missing one wheel. What was left of the statue looked incomplete and idiotic. Most maddening of all, I could not for the life of me find the piece of paper on which I'd written the name of the horrible boy responsible for all this.

I'd scoured every millimeter of my office. I'd even gone personally and ransacked Cynthia's desk, in case she'd carried it off by accident. I'd hired a cleaning company to go over the entire administration building with a fine-tooth comb. Nothing. He was out there somewhere, laughing at me, getting off scot-free.

My wife said I was becoming obsessed with this phantom boy. Maybe so. Lately, I'd been finding excuses to visit Hardcastle Middle School in the hope that I would recognize his cocky sneering face somewhere. But I never saw him. It was as if the culprit didn't go to school there anymore. If only I had the name . . .

Irrationally, I began shuffling papers on my desk. It had been right here!

Cynthia tottered in on her high heels. "Dr. Schultz, I have the first progress report on the new Human Growth and Development project at the Academy.

The special expert is named Katie Patterson, and she's the sister of one of the students, a boy named Don—"

"Just put it on my desk," I interrupted, still peering into drawers. Wasn't that the definition of insanity? Doing the same thing over and over again, and expecting a different result?

I had to get a grip on my nerves. I had duties to perform, and bringing this boy to justice was only one of them. Case in point: The relocated Hardcastle Middle School Valentine Dance was tonight. This would be the first time it had ever taken place off campus, *and* the first time that outside students were being included. We were infinitely proud of our high achievers at the Academy for Scholastic Distinction, but many of them weren't the most socially adept young people. I wanted to be on hand to make sure everything ran smoothly.

And I mustn't forget to make contact with this Mrs. Patterson so I could express the gratitude of the entire school district. What a wonderful family they must be—the husband serving our country in the military, and she, selflessly helping that one class in its time of need. If only more people were like that.

# UNROCKIN'
## CHLOE GARFINKLE
## IQ: 159

*<<Hypothesis: I have the perfect wardrobe—*
*for milking a cow.>>*

No, that was more than a hypothesis. It was cold, hard fact, backed up by the pathetic reality of the contents of my closet. Also feeding chickens, pulling weeds, driving a combine harvester, and other farm chores. What I didn't have was anything to wear to the Valentine Dance.

It wasn't exactly a shocker. Sad to say, I'd never been

to anything like this before. Almost fourteen years old, and the only real party I'd attended was the kind where your parents are there and you have to waltz with your cousin, the bowlegged one with the giant Adam's apple.

Don't get me wrong. I was psyched. I was *beyond* psyched. To me, this was far more than another school's shindig we'd been invited to crash. This was a chance for us to prove an important hypothesis in front of the staff and students of the biggest middle school in town:

<<*Hypothesis: Being gifted doesn't automatically make people social outcasts.*>>

True, some of us *were* social outcasts—Noah Youkilis came to mind. But regular schools had those too. We were no different from the rest of humanity. And we were going to show that we were every bit as capable of having a good time.

All thanks to Donovan Curtis.

Obviously, I understood that Donovan hadn't made any of this happen directly. He couldn't possibly have destroyed the Hardcastle gym, forcing them to move the dance to ours. Nobody was capable of shaping human events like that.

Yet the minute he'd walked into Oz's homeroom

that day, I knew things were about to change. I could feel it in the air; smell it in the wind—of course, that might have been the sulfur fumes from the chemistry lab down the hall. It was almost as if the gods of Normal had sent us their messenger as a sign that our geekdom was coming to an end.

Donovan was almost too normal. I'd heard the rumors around school about an unqualified kid at the Academy. It wasn't hard to identify this newbie who didn't have what it took. It might have been just gossip. Some of us were so hypercompetitive that it killed us to admit anybody else could be the real deal.

From what I'd seen of Donovan, though, there might have been an element of truth to the gossip. It pained me to say it. I liked him a lot, and he'd made a huge contribution to our robotics team, in spite of very limited knowledge of the subject. Best of all, he'd found a way for us to fulfill our Human Growth and Development requirement—something that helped him not at all. He was doing it purely for us.

He was wonderful. But was he gifted?

I wanted to believe it. I tried *so hard*. Yet in my heart of hearts, I knew the answer.

Back to the matter at hand: What to wear? The only guidelines from the school stated that attire couldn't be "inappropriate." That meant no T-shirts with bad language, torn jeans, or miniskirts that could double as headbands. One look in my closet told me that my entire wardrobe was inappropriate. There was nothing that would get me in trouble with the teachers, but everything was so drab. My shirts were all plaid, which doesn't exactly scream party, unless there's a lumberjack theme.

I finally settled on the dress I had worn to my aunt Julie's wedding. It was definitely over the top for a school dance, so I made it more casual by adding a plain black cardigan. I considered wearing sneakers instead of the fancy shoes that went with the outfit, but I couldn't tell if the combination would be funky or just plain stupid. I went to the Academy for Scholastic Distinction, not the one for Fashion Sense.

Makeup was the next hurdle. I thought back to those girls in the mall—the ones hanging out with Donovan and the two boys named Daniel. They'd been wearing tons of makeup. It looked great on them, but if I tried it, for sure I'd paint myself up like Bozo the clown. In the end, I opted for light mascara and a hint of blush—my complexion can be a little pale from too much time in the library.

"You look beautiful!" my dad declared emotionally.

<<*Hypothesis: The compliment loses credibility in direct proportion to how closely related you are to the speaker.*>>

We headed for school. There was a traffic jam on the circular drive. Kids were swarming from all directions, alone and in groups, arriving by car, bike, skateboard, scooter, and on foot. The Academy was small, but Hardcastle Middle had nine hundred students, and it looked like this was going to be a huge turnout. I felt a renewed buzz of excitement, followed by a severe bout of anxiety. By the time we got to the front door, I already knew that my outfit was totally wrong. Most of the girls were wearing either jeans or short skirts, with sneakers or sandals despite the cold weather.

In the end, though, nothing could overpower my exhilaration. Now, barely a few months shy of eighth-grade graduation, I was attending my first middle school dance. I finally had an answer for all those people who said, "Get a life." I was getting one.

Amazingly, I made it into the gym attracting only a few strange looks, so I guess I wasn't as overdressed as I'd feared. The place was about a third full, and kids were pouring in, chattering happily, ready for a good time. The decorations caught the eye first. I don't want to be unkind, but they were really lame—hearts and cupids, lots of streamers, pink, red, and silver everywhere. Hardcastle had done the whole setup—if they'd put us in charge of it, I'm sure we could have come up with something a little more creative. But maybe that was the point.

<<*Hypothesis: Not everything needs to be measured by gifted standards.*>>

Tonight was supposed to be about kicking back and cutting loose a little. Too bad I was doing it in a dorky party dress.

The music was loud—really loud. Feel-it-in-your-molars loud. People were already dancing. Another problem: I didn't know how to do *that* either—not the way they were doing it, anyway.

<<*Hypothesis: The scientific method applies to everything, dancing included.*>>

In other words, if I studied it hard enough, I could catch up.

I only saw a few kids from the Academy, mostly because they seemed to be hiding. They lurked in corners, or in the shadow of the deejay booth. The way they goggled at our guests, you'd think we'd been invaded by Huns who were presently sacking the school. The Hardcastle kids were brasher than us, wilder, and more confident. The boys were a lot more physical—at any given time, 40 percent of them were engaged in shoving one another. And they outnumbered us ten-to-one.

I spotted Oz right away. He wasn't with the other chaperones. He circulated among his own students, urging them to mingle. He would have had a better chance getting Abigail to impale herself on a fence post. I caught her attention, and she gave me a beseeching look—the kind you turn on the helicopter pilot who's coming to save you from drowning. Trying to set a positive example of the sort of hosts Oz expected us to be, I turned to the boy standing next to me and said, "Great turnout. Are all the Hardcastle parties this crowded?"

He didn't hear me. The pounding beat was so loud that my words died less than an inch from my lips. I repeated it, shouting this time.

He shot me a smirk and I leaned in to catch his reply.

"You getting married in that dress?"

And before I could answer, he was yanked away through the crowd by a group of friends.

"Hi, Chloe!"

The voice wasn't any louder than mine, but its piercing quality cut through the music like a fire siren.

If I was worried about being improperly dressed, Noah took all that pressure onto his slender shoulders.

His outfit defied description, but in the gifted program we're encouraged to try. He was shirtless, his upper body covered only by a sparkling sequined vest. His pants were black tights, which made his skinny legs even skinnier. You couldn't see much of them, though, because he had on knee-high red leather boots that must have weighed thirty pounds each. It was a miracle he could even walk. Mirrored sunglasses concealed his eyes, and his unstylish brush cut was covered with a red do-rag.

I was horrified. "Noah, what are you wearing?"

"I borrowed the boots and the vest from my mom," he enthused. "When the Angel of Death fought Kid Nitro at the Royal Rumble, this is just like what he wore."

"Yeah, but this is a dance, not a wrestling match."

He shrugged. "Oz said we had to dress up."

I had no answer to that. But I sure wanted to be there when Oz got a gander at what Noah thought "dress up" looked like.

<<*Hypothesis: As a space fills with people, the air inside warms, approaching 98.6 degrees Fahrenheit, the body temperature of the crowd.*>>

I began to regret my cardigan. I was going to be sweaty, not just overdressed. It was getting really packed, to the point where glimpses of the floor were rare.

Lost in the wall-to-wall students, I was no longer able to survey the entire party. Instead, I'd catch the occasional familiar face amid the forest of heads and shoulders. I located Latrell by the back wall—it seemed like Oz was working on him to ask someone to dance. Kevin and Jacey were hanging together for mutual support in this alien environment. I thought I saw Donovan once, but it turned out to be somebody else. Maybe he wasn't going to show up.

All my nervousness returned in any icy wave. There was something isolating about being smothered by strangers, even in a familiar setting like your own school gym.

As the crush tightened around me, I felt myself swept along with the movement of the crowd. I was afraid at first, until I recognized the strange combination of motions that pushed me back and forth.

Dancing! As far as I could see in every direction, bodies gyrated, heads were thrown back, hands swayed through the air. I tried to bulldoze my way out of the group, but flailing arms and swinging hips jostled me. I kept stumbling—but there was more to it than that.

I was stumbling *in perfect time to the music!*

I raised my hands and moved my feet, following the pounding bass.

*<<Hypothesis: Intentional or not, movement to a beat = dancing.>>*

I risked a furtive glance at my neighbors. No *What-do-you-think-you're-doing?* glares; no gathering lynch mob. I cranked up the energy level, rollicking at light speed.

I—Chloe Garfinkle of the Academy for Scholastic Distinction—was one of the crowd, letting it all hang out at a major middle school bash.

This was the greatest night of my life!

# UNTRUSTWORTHY

## DONOVAN CURTIS
## IQ: 112

This was the worst night of my life.

Bad enough to be banished to the Island of Misfit Toys without having everybody you know come and visit you there. I'd have given anything to take a pass on this dance. I'd even offered to do an extra-credit project for Oz. He'd just regarded me sadly, as if to say, what could I possibly deliver that would be good enough? Showing up was the only thing I could do every bit as well as Abigail or Noah.

Speaking of Noah, he looked like—holy hamburgers, what *did* he look like? It was almost comforting that I had no idea. If I understood his getup, it might have meant part of me was inside that bizarro world.

I saw the smirks and overheard some of the nasty remarks directed toward kids like Noah and Abigail, who was dressed for the National Spelling Bee. Or Latrell, who had asked at least half a dozen girls to dance, and had been shot down by all of them. If Oz thought this would be confidence building, he was nuts!

*"Pa-a-arty!!!"*

It wasn't easy to drown out the sound system, but Sanderson bellowed it right in my ear.

Nussbaum was beside him. It was a bad omen. "What a night, huh, Donovan? Lot of hotties in this crowd! Her, for instance."

I followed his pointing finger, expecting to see Heather or Deirdre. No, it was Abigail in the crosshairs. Oz had her dancing, which she was accomplishing with two locked knee joints. I've seen heads of lettuce with more rhythm. She moved like a stilt walker. The things some people do for their straight A's!

"Cut it out," I growled.

"This party rocks!" Sanderson declared. "You can

feel the brainpower buzzing around like radio waves. I'm getting smarter just standing here."

"That's not how it works," Nussbaum scoffed. "The higher up you wear your belt, that's your genius level. If I buckle mine around my forehead, do you think I could go to school here just like the great Donovan Curtis?"

I groaned. "Hilarious, guys. Now, go find—"

My voice trailed off. Mr. Osborne had left Abigail, and was venturing on in search of somebody else to annoy. Now the Daniels were pushing through the crowd, heading right for her.

"Come back here!" Who was I kidding? I'd never make myself heard over the music. And if they did hear me, would they listen? Fat chance.

There were only two Daniels, yet they seemed to swarm Abigail, surrounding her, smiling, being charming, all the while smirking and rolling their eyes. Their audience was everybody—the Hardcastle kids, anyway. The Daniels got her dancing again, comically stiff-legged.

I should have been laughing myself. What did I care about Abigail Lee? The girl hated me, and I wasn't too fond of her, either. But the whole attitude—the idea that the gifted kids were here for the entertainment of the cool people—made me sick. It was bad enough now, with Abigail treating the Daniels like muggers. But if they managed to win her over, convince her that they liked her—*that* would be major-league humiliation.

I blasted through the gathering crowd, outflanked the Daniels, and grabbed Abigail's wrist with a grip that must have hurt at least a little. I don't even know what I said. Something like, "You're dancing with *me* now."

If she viewed the Daniels as muggers, the look she gave me was Voldemort-worthy. I didn't care. She had to be saved, undeserving as she was.

Nussbaum got in my face. "What's your problem, Donovan?"

"She's in my homeroom," I replied through clenched teeth. "I get first dibs."

"Manners, dude! We're guests!"

Abigail was watching all this through her thick round glasses, her uncomfortable expression turning to bewilderment. She was brilliant, but all the IQ points in the world wouldn't help her in a situation like this. It must have seemed like three guys fighting over her—something I guarantee had never happened before. Not on this planet.

She tried to sidestep me and return to the Daniels. Talk about a blow to your self-esteem—I was being *dumped* by Abigail! That had to be an all-time low! I stuck with the plan, though, taking her hand and twirling her around—a maneuver she executed with the grace of someone who was being handcuffed by police.

Luckily, the Daniels saw the chaperones watching and retreated before Abigail could get back to them. Or maybe it was unlucky—it left me dancing with her. I was stuck too. I couldn't very well chase away two guys, and then blow her off the minute they were gone. It was pretty ridiculous, when you think about it. I didn't even like these school parties, and here I'd gone to great lengths to saddle myself doing my unfavorite thing with my unfavorite person. At least the Daniels had retreated. I saw them over by the drink table, now schmoozing some other girl—one who was a lot more their type. She was tall with long legs and a really cute face. A little overdressed, but she made it work. A cut above your standard eighth-grade girl who got caught downwind of the makeup factory explosion.

I did a double take.

That was no hottie; that was *Chloe!* Plaid-flannel

Chloe! I barely recognized her! Man, she looked different! And not just different-different! Different-*awesome!*

It made sense. This party was a huge deal to her. Of course she'd go all out.

And now the Daniels were going to lob a grenade into her night.

I snagged Noah by the sparkle vest, and yanked him over to Abigail. "No problem, Noah. Of course you can cut in. Have a good time, you two."

And I was off like a shot, plowing through the tightly packed attendees. By the time I'd reached Chloe, she was in her glory, basking in the attention of two "normal" guys. Sarcasm intended.

I grabbed each Daniel by the back of the collar and pulled them away from her.

Chloe was horrified. "Donovan, what are you doing?"

I decided to be more honest with Chloe than I'd been with Abigail. "I know these clowns."

"I know them too, remember? From the mall?"

"Beat it, Donovan," Nussbaum urged. "You know when they say 'party pooper?' That's you right now."

I'd never be able to explain it to her—that they were only building her up so they could drop her over a cliff and walk away laughing. So I just kept hold of them by the scruffs of their necks, and marched them through the exit.

Chloe was following us. "What's the matter with you, Donovan? You can't treat people like that!" Her anger was a microclimate. I could feel the heat all around me. Another satisfied customer.

I dragged the Daniels where she couldn't follow us—into the boys' bathroom. The door gonged shut behind us, leaving her in midsentence.

Nussbaum surveyed the plumbing fixtures. "Look at that toilet! That's got to be the smartest toilet I've ever seen. You could come in here an idiot, and leave a genius!"

"And you would have done your business too," added Sanderson helpfully. "You know—if you had to go. It's a win-win situation."

"All right, guys," I sighed. "I get it. You don't like the gifted school very much. Neither do I. But for reasons you know very well, I'm stuck here."

"I pity you," Nussbaum commiserated. "These people! Did you catch that guy with the vest and the boots? What is he—a Christmas tree ornament?"

"That guy," I told him, "is smarter than everybody else at the Academy put together, with the rest of us thrown in for good measure. He could probably devise a way to kill you without looking away from his YouTube videos."

"Him?" Nussbaum hooted. "Don't make me laugh!"

"They're just people," I pleaded. "So what if they're a little nerdier than the rest of us? I know you came here to make trouble. Please don't."

"You're no fun anymore," Sanderson complained. "The old Donovan would be with us a hundred percent. You'd pants the vest guy, and take the kneeless chick on *Dancing with the Stars*. And the good-looking one—"

"She wasn't *that* good," Nussbaum put in critically.

"You could whack her with a branch so that she rolls down and smashes something. It wouldn't be the first time."

I sighed. "Go home. This isn't the place for you."

"Now I'm insulted," Nussbaum drawled. "We come all the way across town to visit your smarty-pants school, and you try to kick us out? Where's your hospitality? You didn't show us your locker. You didn't show us your homeroom. You didn't even show us your famous robot. We deserve better than that."

I looked at him skeptically. "You're interested in the robot?"

"Interested? Man, I'm a robot enthusiast! I saw *The Terminator*, like, twenty times!"

I hesitated. "If I show you Tin Man, do you promise to leave the Academy kids alone?"

Sanderson snapped the two-finger salute. "Scout's honor."

"You were never a scout!" sneered Nussbaum. "They threw you out! They threw us all out when Donovan burned down the tent."

I couldn't suppress a smile. "It said 'fireproof' on the box."

"Maybe that meant the *box* was fireproof," Nussbaum conceded.

We all laughed. At the time, it hadn't been funny, but it was pretty funny now.

"I'll show you the robot."

Homeroom 107 wasn't far from the gym—just two turns down dim hallways past the custodial offices and a couple of science labs. The door was closed but unlocked. I opened it, and turned on the lights to reveal the organized chaos that was the robotics program.

"Whoa!" breathed Sanderson. "Paging Dr. Frankenstein!"

Funny, I was used to the place. But to the Daniels, it might as well have had bubbling test tubes and jagged forks of electricity dancing up Jacob's ladders. Equipment was piled on every surface, components and spare parts lay strewn like candy wrappers, and odd instruments and tools hung from the walls. There were even "cobwebs" of multicolored wires suspended from the ceiling and stretched all over.

"So where's the robot?" asked Nussbaum.

I pointed to Tin Man at the center of it all. "Star of our show."

"What? That?" Sanderson exclaimed in disbelief. "That's just a metal box with a picture of some old guy eating a banana!"

"That's Einstein, Einstein!" Nussbaum exploded.

"He's old, isn't he?"

"No, he's dead! Sheesh! How stupid can you get?"

Sanderson gestured at the jungle of wires and technology that surrounded us. "Donovan, you understand all this . . . stuff?"

"I don't understand *any* of it," I replied honestly. "Even Mr. Osborne doesn't get much more than half. That's why it takes a team. We've got mechanical people, electronics people, computer people, hydraulics people, and pneumatics people."

"Which are you?" Nussbaum prodded.

"I downloaded the pictures," I admitted ruefully. "And I'm good with the controller—years of practice with video games."

They seemed dissatisfied with this explanation, like I was holding something back. "Guys, you of all people know why I'm at this school. Do you think I got into the Academy for my brain, and then busted up the gym on purpose so I'd have a cover story as an excuse to come here every day? I'm hiding! I know it's not going to last forever, but I have to keep it going at least until the heat dies down. My family doesn't have the kind of money it would take to fix that gym. Or to pay for lawyers if we get sued! So please don't make it any harder than it already is."

They took pity on me. It must have been the lab that did the trick. Maybe it finally sunk in how unfun it was to be the only mental turkey in a school of soaring eagles.

By the time we got back to the gym, the dance was completely off the chain. The floor almost moved with the force of hundreds of pounding feet. Bodies were packed in like sardines, the heat and humidity pushing past the tolerance level. The chaperones were trying in vain to thin out the crowd, which had to be far past what the fire marshal would have found acceptable. Whatever food and drink was left had been mashed into a paste and spread as a thin film across the hardwood. The music was so loud that the beat rattled your brain inside the casing of your skull.

Did I mention the smell? Pizza, sweat, and AXE body spray.

Sanderson grabbed Nussbaum. "Let's find Heather and Deirdre!"

"I'll catch up with you guys later," I promised. It was a lie. The only person I intended to catch up with was Mr. Osborne. Once my extra credit was in the bag, I was out of here.

You couldn't push through this crowd any more. You had to be swallowed, the way an amoeba ingests its food. Movement was worth your life. At least twice, the ebb and flow took me out onto the dance floor. At one point, I passed very close to Chloe, who glared at me, still miffed. When I finally spotted Oz, he looked like he now regretted making attendance mandatory for his students. It served him right.

I waved my arm in an attempt to catch his attention, and that was when I recognized the other adult standing beside him, the man who had to be even hotter than the rest of us in his three-piece suit.

Dr. Schultz.

I ducked out of the superintendent's line of sight. He'd never spot me at the crowd's butt level. Being trampled was a small price to pay to remain hidden. Extra credit meant nothing now. All that mattered was escape.

I got down on all fours and crawled, not the most dignified way to leave a party, and definitely not the cleanest. Let me tell you, whether it's the coolest Hardcastle jock, or the dweebiest squint in the Academy, it hurts the same when they're stomping on your fingers. But it was the most efficient way to travel. Pretty soon, I was at the door, home free.

Before I made my break, I gave the madness one last scan. What I saw nearly stopped my heart.

At the very center of the dance floor, the nucleus of the amoeba, a huge tight circle had formed around a small group of dancers. Three of them, to be exact. Daniel Sanderson, Daniel Nussbaum, and Tin Man Metallica Squarepants.

Rage almost blinded me. My "friends" had doubled back to the lab and wheeled the robot right into the riotous pounding heart of the Valentine Dance.

The dilemma was excruciating, and instantly clear. If I went back in there to rescue Tin Man, and Schultz spotted me, my whole world would come crashing down around my ears. What did I care if Tin Man got trashed? It wasn't my robot. It wasn't even my school. The sum total of my contribution to the project was a name and Einstein eating a banana!

No. Not true. I'd made another contribution—the Daniels. If it wasn't for me, those two bottom feeders would never have known that Tin Man even existed. Anything that happened to that poor robot tonight was my fault.

That's when it hit me. I *did* care. Not so much about the robotics team—and definitely not about some bucket of bolts on Mecanum wheels. How many chances did I get to limit the damage of my impulses? Once Atlas's globe is rolling, there's nothing anyone can do to save the gym at the bottom of the hill.

But this was different. Tin Man wasn't wrecked yet. There was still time to make things right.

I pushed back into the gym, jamming my way through dancing torsos. I could see that my trajectory was taking me on a collision course with Oz and— yikes!—Dr. Schultz. The adults had spotted Tin Man and were rushing to the robot. I grabbed a baseball cap off the nearest head, and jammed it low over my face. Why make it easy for the guy to bust me?

Some of my classmates had noticed too. Kevin, Jacey, and Latrell were stuck at various places in the crowd, struggling to reach Tin Man. Abigail was red-faced and screaming, although her cries were inaudible in the general din. Chloe got behind me, riding my wake toward the scene of the crime. We were making progress, but would we get there in time?

At the center of it all, Sanderson was draped over Tin Man's back, rolling the robot to and fro as if slow-dancing with it. Nussbaum had hold of the two forklift arms, and was jitterbugging to his own rhythms. I tackled him to the gym floor, and when he went down, he took one of the arms with him. Triumphantly, he held it over his head, and an enormous cheer rose in the gym.

To my classmates, it meant only one thing: Tin Man was being dismantled.

Kevin and Latrell faced down Sanderson.

*"Get away from Tin Man!"* Kevin bawled.

Problem was, those guys had never been in a fight in their lives, so their body language was completely unfightlike. Latrell couldn't even make a fist properly—he had his thumb pressed *inside* his fingers.

Sanderson took one look at that and laughed in their faces. He stopped laughing, though, when Abigail booted him in the shins.

"Get out of my school, you"—she struggled for just the right put-down—"you *average person!*"

That's when it got ugly. A shoving match broke out. After a few seconds, it was no longer just the Daniels *vs.* the robotics team. The conflict had widened. It was now Hardcastle *vs.* the Academy.

All the resentment, the jealousy, and the bullying attitude toward the gifted program boiled over at that very spot, turning the dance into a free-for-all, with Tin Man caught in the crossfire.

The bloodcurdling shriek was barely human. We all looked up to see Noah Youkilis, poised atop the dee-jay's giant speaker tower, muscles flexed—at least, they would have been if he'd had any. The bizarre pose left no room for interpretation. It was a ridiculous time to notice it, but I finally understood what his outfit was supposed to be. He was a WWE wrestler, just like the ones he'd seen on YouTube, only fifty times skinnier.

And before everybody's horrified eyes, he did exactly what they do on *SmackDown*. He launched himself off the tower in a spectacular dive into the fray. I figured he was dead meat. But his fall was broken by the people he landed on. The crowd swayed, absorbing his impact. Many figures went down. Tin Man was one of them.

Oz looked like he wanted to tear himself in half. I'm pretty sure he couldn't decide whether he should rush to the aid of his fallen student or his fallen robot.

And then, for the first time all night, something intelligent happened. The fire alarm went off. At first I was kind of surprised it wasn't me who did it. It was very much my style. But when I looked over at the wall, the culprit was standing there, still holding on to the lever.

Dr. Schultz. I guess when you're the superintendent, you don't have to worry about getting in trouble.

In the blink of an eye, several hundred kids swarmed the gym door. Hey, I knew an exit strategy when I saw one. I was gone before Schultz could even glance in my direction.

# UNSORRY
## NOAH YOUKILIS
## IQ: 206

For all the eight hundred million videos on YouTube, you had to figure there were at least another eight hundred million that never got filmed.

YouTube had its conundrums too:

*A) The best stuff comes when somebody does something awesome.*

*B) Awesomeness is unpredictable, so it isn't practical to have a camera in hand at all times to capture it.*

Me being the hero of the Valentine Dance, for instance.

One day it might be possible to hardwire a person's optic nerve to a tiny memory chip implanted in the base of the skull. You'd just need a simple internet connection to upload the images to YouTube.

With our best minds focused on curing diseases and stuff like that, I wasn't holding my breath.

Speaking of the dance, Friday night had not been kind to Tin Man. Oh, the scratches could be buffed out, the dents repaired, and the broken forklift arm reattached again. But the motor that ran the lift mechanism had suffered permanent damage, and Oz said our budget for new materials was exhausted.

Abigail was distraught. "But if we don't have a lift mechanism, we'll have to withdraw from the competition!"

This prospect had Jacey so stressed out that she started talking about South American butterfly migrations. If anyone knew more random facts than me, it was Jacey.

But today it was getting on my nerves. "My blunt-trauma anterior epistaxis is better, thank you very much!"

"Who cares about your dumb bloody nose?" Abigail snapped.

"*I* care!" I shot back. "It *really* hurt! I didn't see any of you guys single-handedly rescuing Tin Man in the riot." For some reason, I was getting no credit at all for sacrificing my body. If it isn't on YouTube, it might as well have never happened.

"More like you *caused* the riot," put in Latrell sourly. "When you jumped on everybody from the top of the deejay booth."

"It wasn't a jump," I explained through clenched teeth. "It was a takedown. It was a textbook wrestling move."

Chloe turned to Donovan. "Your two friends named Daniel—why did they do that? Why would they want to mess with our robot?"

Donovan shrugged. "A lot of kids have an attitude about the gifted program. And those guys definitely have an attitude now that I'm in it. Look at this place—Hardcastle's an ancient ruin compared to here. They've got about a sixteenth of the stuff we do. They may call us nerds, but it's pretty cool having your own robot."

I didn't agree. A robot wasn't cool; it was just complicated. Like the LEGO Star Wars Imperial Snow Walker. (*Consumer Reports* said that not even a genius could put one together. They were wrong. I'd already assembled six.)

In my opinion, having a robot was a lot less interesting than having a riot. Riots were unforeseeable and chaotic—very YouTube-like.

Oz tried everything to get money for a new motor. He requested funds from the athletic budget, but he couldn't convince them that Tin Man was more important than badminton. He even took apart his own lawnmower in the hope that the engine would be the right size. It wasn't—and now the lawnmower won't go back together again. Latrell has to go to his house to fix it.

"Couldn't we raise the money?" Chloe pleaded. "Sell candy bars or something? We can't drop out!"

Oz shrugged unhappily. "There's simply not enough time to set up something like that. The robotics meet is in three weeks."

Donovan was even quieter than usual during the entire class. Tin Man's outer shell was completely covered with graphics by now, so there was nothing for him to do but drive. And with the lift system inoperable, there was no sense driving the robot anywhere.

Finally, when the period was over, he gathered us in

the hall. "I think I've found us a spare motor."

Abigail began jumping up and down. "What? What? *Where?*"

"In the custodial office," he explained. "It runs one of the floor polishers. You'd know better than me, but I'm pretty sure it'll fit Tin Man."

"How did you reach that conclusion?" I inquired. "Did you measure the unit itself, or are you thinking of the size and location of the key components and connections?"

"I guessed," he admitted a little sheepishly.

We stared at him in amazement. After all, *we* were the ones who had created Tin Man, not Donovan. It had taken design, programming, electronics, hydraulics, pneumatics, and mechanical engineering. No guessing.

Donovan explained. "There are two ways it can go. It can either fit or not fit."

"A probability analysis?" I mused.

He shrugged. "I can't say for sure it'll work. But I *guarantee* that if we don't at least try, that bucket of bolts will have no lift motor. What have we got to lose?"

Chloe had a practical question. "And the custodians are letting us have it? They're always so crabby."

Donovan grinned. "They're really great guys."

He insisted that we had to pick the engine up immediately, even before going to the cafeteria to eat. We'd all learned to trust Donovan for one reason or another, so we went along with it. But when we arrived at the custodial office, it was deserted.

"Where is everybody?" I asked.

"At lunch," Donovan replied.

"But where's the motor?" Abigail persisted.

"It's in the floor polisher," Donovan explained, producing a screwdriver. "Where else?"

It was all beginning to make sense. The custodians weren't *giving* us anything. We were *taking*.

Abigail was furious. "We can't steal their motor!"

"It's not *their* motor," Donovan lectured. "It's the school's motor. It's also the school's robot."

I'd seen things like this on YouTube, but never could I have imagined being a part of it in real life. It took Latrell several tense minutes to dismantle the polisher and remove the engine.

"Put the cover back on," Donovan instructed. "We don't want them to see it's missing."

Abigail was practically hysterical. "Don't you think they're going to notice when they try to polish the floor?"

I was the lookout. It was my job to give the code word if I saw one of the custodians coming.

"Pythagoras!" I hissed.

Donovan yanked the screwdriver out of Latrell's hand and tossed it out of view while kicking the floor polisher under a workbench. In the same motion, he herded everybody into the supply closet, jammed in after them, and slammed the door. I'd never seen anybody move so fast.

"It's okay," I called. "I was just testing."

Donovan came out of the closet and fixed me with twin lasers. "Do that again and they'll be watching your funeral on YouTube."

I admired Donovan, but he scared me sometimes.

Sneaking back to the robotics lab with our prize was the most exciting experience I could remember, even better than my big takedown at the dance. I knew a lot about the effects of adrenaline on the human body, but that was different than actually feeling my heart pounding against my rib cage. Fear mixed with exhilaration, plus the notion that, at any second, we could get caught. It was almost as if I hadn't really been alive until Donovan showed up at the Academy.

Oz was ecstatic. "Where did you guys get this?"

It didn't bother him at all that nobody answered.

The polisher's motor was a little bit bigger than the broken one. "We'll have to reconfigure it to run on battery power," Oz advised. "And the extra weight might slow us down a little."

"But we'll have a lot more juice," Donovan put in.

"We don't need more juice," Abigail pointed out. "The task is to pick up inflatable rings that weigh practically nothing."

Oz had a different opinion. "We had a real problem, and we found a way to solve it. That's what the robotics program is all about."

The next day the floor looked a little dull and neglected. But Tin Man was back online.

The rumor started with Kevin Amari, who dropped the bomb in the cafeteria.

"I overheard Oz telling Mr. Del Rio that they're going to retest Donovan for the Academy."

Chloe choked on a celery stalk. "What? Why?"

"You're kidding, right?" Abigail said flatly. "It's obvious to everybody he isn't gifted. They gave him a few weeks to prove himself, and he didn't."

"He's proved himself a million different ways," Chloe argued.

"Because he stole a motor?" she retorted.

"Maybe," I said defiantly. "If you give the robotics team a motor, we can do anything with it. But if you ask us to *get* a motor, we'd all be dead in the water."

"And what about Human Growth and Development?" Chloe demanded.

"It doesn't matter," Abigail insisted. "They can't just keep on letting him flunk."

"They do it with me," I muttered. "I'd love to be retested. I'd show them the true meaning of *flunk*."

Abigail stared me down. "Come on. You can't seriously be saying that you don't see any difference between Donovan's situation and your personal weirdness. Your IQ is higher than his by at least a whole person."

"We *need* him," I insisted. "He's more important than any of us."

"Please! One of us couldn't learn how to work a controller? Or download stupid pictures to put on him?"

"We could do it," I gritted. "But we'd do it *wrong*!" It was impossible to explain what I meant. Donovan was a human version of YouTube. Click on him, and you might get Einstein eating a banana, or a heisted motor, or a robot driver, or a Human Growth and Development credit. It was like rolling a die with an infinite number of sides.

Chloe looked thoughtful. "Maybe he'll pass the retest."

There was an awkward silence as that idea went down like a lead balloon.

"He's working really hard," she argued. "You know—for him."

"Exactly." Abigail was triumphant. "His grades are *awful*. He might be trying, but what does that mean? That this is the best he can do?"

"You don't have to look so happy about it," I told her.

"What about his science project?" Latrell suggested. "He's burning the midnight oil on that."

"Right," Abigail agreed sarcastically. "Googling dog facts and taking pictures of the family pet."

Kevin had a suggestion. "We could ask Oz to delay the test. At least until after Human Growth and Development. And by then the robotics meet will be done too."

Chloe was annoyed. "A little selfish, don't you think?"

"Besides," Latrell told him, "big-time colleges bench superstars who are household names because their grade point averages drop below 2.0. He's toast."

"*We're* toast," groaned Kevin. "If we go to the meet

without Donovan, Cold Spring Harbor is going to run all over us again."

"Not necessarily," Abigail said defiantly. Even she didn't sound convinced.

Jacey seemed to be bursting with something to say, but when we turned to her, she just mumbled, "Nothing. I was thinking about those subatomic particles that travel faster than light. I guess it doesn't help Donovan to know Einstein was probably wrong."

"He could study," Chloe suggested. And when snorts of laughter greeted this, she added, "We could help him study."

"Or," I put in thoughtfully, "one of us could take the test for him, and make sure he passes."

"Oh, right," scoffed Kevin. "Like no one's going to notice it's the wrong person."

"The test is on a computer, remember? All we'd have to do is gain remote control of his mouse and change just enough of his answers to put him over the top."

Abigail was horrified. "That's cheating! Do you know how much trouble you could get in for that?"

I was intrigued. "How much?" In my case, they'd probably just take the opportunity to give me extra credit. The whole system was against me.

"If you get caught doing something like that,"

Abigail warned, voice rising, "it would go on your permanent record! You'd never get into Stanford or MIT with a black mark like that!"

"Really?" I asked.

Abigail rolled her eyes. "For you, they'd just add twenty grand to your scholarship."

Chloe shook her head sadly. "I feel bad for Donovan. He's a really good person. I got mad at him at the dance, but now I know he was only trying to protect me. I wish we could help him. You know, legally."

I realized something about Donovan then. We were two sides of the same coin. He was struggling to stay in the gifted program, and I was struggling to get out.

# UNTESTED

## DONOVAN CURTIS
## IQ: 112

oah Youkilis gave Daniel Sanderson a black eye at the dance on Friday night. It happened when Noah did that Wrestlemania dive from the deejay's speaker tower. Somehow, he must have kicked Sanderson in the face with his mother's red leather boots. I'm sure it was an accident. Noah wouldn't hurt a fly.

Technically, it was all my fault. I'm the one who turned Noah on to YouTube, and that's where he discovered professional wrestling. I didn't feel bad, though, because Sanderson totally had it coming. My only regret was that Noah couldn't have gotten Nussbaum with the other foot.

Trust me, I didn't hear any of this from the Daniels themselves. I told my parents and Katie that, if those guys called or came by, I was officially not at home.

"But why, Donnie? They're your best friends."

"I thought they were my friends when I showed them the robot," I replied. "But then they went behind my back and wheeled it into the gym, so a thousand idiots could use it as a punching clown!"

"What do you care about their robot?" Katie challenged.

"I'm the driver," I argued. "We're like the Lone Ranger and his horse."

Her eyes narrowed. "Any idiot can work a joystick. What else did you do on the project? Did you help build it?"

"Part of it."

She was unconvinced. "What part?"

"The exterior," I said stubbornly.

"You can't even make Kraft dinner," Katie accused. "Where would you learn how to build a sophisticated piece of technology?"

"It's not about the robot; it's about the Daniels," I insisted. "Those guys think they can treat the gifted kids like they don't measure up as humans. You can't push people around in front of a dozen chaperones, so they took it out on Tin Man. I'm not talking to them."

Mom respected my wishes but, on Wednesday, Nussbaum took a picture of Sanderson's face on his cell phone, and texted it to Katie. She'd always had a soft spot for the Daniels, if you can imagine Katie having a soft spot for anybody. Anyway, when she showed me the picture, I did a double take. Sanderson looked like he'd been hit by a train, not a half-pint YouTube-obsessed genius. What a shiner! His eye wasn't just black. It was purple and yellow and green, and a few shades I didn't know the names of.

"*Noah* did that?" my sister exclaimed in amazement.

"He comes across like a dork, but he's got killer moves." And his mom had killer footwear.

In the end, my conscience won out, and I headed over to Sanderson's. If the Daniels were texting my sister, they were really angling for a visit. Which meant they probably wanted to apologize. I guess I had to go over there and let them.

Sanderson might have been suffering, but it hadn't

stopped him from milking this injury for all it was worth. He had Deirdre and Heather over there, holding his hand and refreezing ice packs for his poor eye.

Nussbaum was on the scene too, limping a little just in case there was any sympathy spillover from the girls. If I thought I was going to get an apology, I was mistaken. Instead, everyone started talking about the night of the dance, and "that bully." I swear, I had absolutely no idea who they were talking about. The only bullies in that gym had been the Daniels themselves.

"What bully?" I asked finally.

"You know," said Sanderson. "The one who hit me. That bodybuilder in the wrestling outfit."

I was blown away. "With the red boots?"

Sanderson gave me a beseeching look. He was determined to prove in front of the girls that he'd been brutalized by a huge monster, and he expected me to back him up.

He picked the wrong person on the wrong day. "Noah Youkilis could lose a fight to a spiderweb. He's six inches shorter than you, and he weighs about as much as your cat."

"He's a black belt in tae kwon do!"

Deirdre spoke up. "You guys in the Academy may

think you're special just because you're smart. But you can't go around punching people. This Noah delinquent could be kicked out of school for what he did!"

I laughed. "Noah? He couldn't get kicked out of school for murder!"

The Daniels stuck to their guns though. Every time they mentioned Noah, he got bigger and meaner, and trained by a more secret paramilitary organization. As soon as the girls were gone, though, they offered a little remorse for kidnapping the robot—in a Daniels sort of way.

"Yeah, I guess it was kind of uncool," Nussbaum murmured. "But you should have seen the look on your face!"

"*Totally* worth it," agreed Sanderson. "At least till that little ninja cold-cocked me. And by the way, thanks for nothing for having my back with Heather and Deirdre a minute ago."

I laughed mirthlessly. "You'd better pray they never get a look at Noah close up."

"*He'd* better pray he never gets a look at *me*!" Sanderson promised darkly.

"That's quite a crowd you hang with over at the genius school," Nussbaum observed. "You never told us plaid shirt was the normal one."

For some reason, that really got to me. "You know, a few of those kids are so smart that we're not even smart enough to understand how smart they are. So leave them alone. And definitely leave their robot alone."

"We were just fooling around," Nussbaum mumbled. "We used to know a kid who did stuff like that all the time—a kid named Donovan Curtis."

I almost forgave them, because they definitely had a point. What were a few bumps and scrapes on Tin Man compared to the wreckage I'd visited on the Hardcastle gym? They were the same old Daniels. I was the one who was different.

Besides, with my big retest coming up, you had to figure I'd be back at Hardcastle Middle School before too long. I was going to need some friends there.

I approached the upcoming testing the way a death row inmate approaches the date of his execution. Reluctantly, and with feet dragging.

It was kind of touching how many of my robotics classmates offered to help me study, coach me. With the exception of Abigail, who was planning to relish my failure, everyone seemed to be pulling for me. A lot of it might have been because of Katie, or because

I was the best person to drive Tin Man at the robotics meet. But I like to think some of it was because they'd accepted me as one of them—even though I was so far below them intellectually that I needed a telescope to see the soles of their shoes.

Chloe offered to work with me at least twenty times. She was kind of offended that I kept blowing her off. I couldn't make her understand that it was nothing personal. I probably should have just come out and told her, point-blank, that I had even less chance of comprehending what she knew than I had of passing the test. When I finally caved, and let her help me with the math portion, she talked so far over my head that all I could hear was airy whispers. And every time she tried to dumb it down, it became a little bit harder to understand.

When we were done, she looked at me in genuine alarm. "Oh, wow, Donovan. What are you going to do?"

Translation: *Stick a fork in me. I'm done.*

I shrugged. "I'll put in some time tonight. Maybe it'll all click."

She wasn't buying it. "You need more than a click. You need a *miracle*. Maybe we should get Noah to tutor you. He'd do it. Any one of us would!"

I laughed bravely. "If I can't understand you, a study session with Noah would make my head explode."

Funny—even though Chloe was back to her plaid shirts and baggy jeans, I kept seeing her as she'd looked all dressed up at the party. The idea of her finding out exactly how smart I wasn't had become kind of sad to me. I even had a plan for cleaning out my locker after school hours so there would be less chance of her witnessing my disgrace. One day I'd be there, the next I'd be gone. After a few weeks, maybe somebody would say, "Remember that guy who used to go here for a while? What was his name again?" No one would have the answer except Noah, and he would pretend he didn't. Eventually, all that would remain of my time at the Academy would be the faded pictures peeling off of Tin Man. And by then, no one would be able to recall who had put them there.

On the big day, things were quieter than usual in the robotics lab. Nobody would meet my eyes, not even Oz. As my homeroom teacher and faculty advisor, it had to have been him who recommended me for retesting. He probably felt like an axe murderer this morning. Even Tin Man seemed a little slumped over and depressed, although that might have been the extra weight of the floor-polisher motor.

I had one last card to play. I marched up to Oz and placed a thick folder on the teacher's desk. He regarded me questioningly, and I pointed to the title: "Chow Chows: A Special Breed." Below it was a large photograph of Beatrice, flaked out on her side, looking about 90 percent comatose. To my long list of regrets, I should add the fact that I had waited to take the picture until she was too far gone to be alert and alive.

"My science project," I announced.

"Shouldn't this go to Mr. Holman?" he asked.

"I thought maybe you could hand it in for me," I explained lamely, "since I might miss science today while I'm taking the test."

My pathetically desperate Technicolor hope was that he'd see this fabulous project, realize that I was working my butt off, and cancel the retest. But he didn't even open it. "Sure," he said very absently, and glanced at his watch.

Noah drifted by the desk. "Good picture," he commented. "Interesting idea to use a pregnant dog."

The earth lurched. "Pregnant?" I rasped. "Beatrice?"

"Of course." The young genius pointed out the features that had gotten by me and my entire family. "Note the distended belly, the prominent nipples, and the languid posture. Weren't you paying attention in Human Growth and Development when we compared human pregnancies to those of other mammals?"

I couldn't even respond, so rocked was I by this news. Wait till Katie got a load of this one. Her tank commander husband was expecting not one blessed event, but two! Brad's sainted mother must have let Beatrice run wild—and look what had happened! Later, when the dog started acting funny, Fanny had dumped her on us so she wouldn't have to take the blame.

My project—the one that was going to prove I belonged at the Academy—didn't mention a single word about pregnancy. So it was all stupid.

I snatched up my folder. "I just need to make a few last-minute adjustments—"

At that moment, the PA system crackled to life. "Mr. Osborne, would you bring Donovan Curtis to the library. . . ."

"Ten minutes!" I pleaded.

I don't know if the voice heard me, but the announcement continued, "Immediately, please."

That's where it was going to happen—the library. They would sit me down in front of a computer, and feed me questions I didn't have the answers to. In the end, it wouldn't matter that my chow chow project was a disaster. I wouldn't be in the gifted program much longer.

I squared my shoulders to my classmates. "Later, guys." But what I meant was, *Good-bye.*

They looked devastated. Even Abigail seemed a lot less happy than I'd expected her to be. Either that, or she was holding off on the celebration until I was officially out.

The walk to the far side of the building had never seemed shorter.

"The test will be coming over the internet from the state department of education," Oz explained as I took my seat. "Don't be nervous. It's not meant to trick you; it's meant to let you show what you know."

That was not at all comforting.

The state department of education made me cool my heels. I sat in stiff-necked misery, sweating. The bell rang. Homeroom was over. I heard the sounds of moving feet in the hall. Life was going on for everyone but me.

Oz gripped my shoulder. "We're all rooting for you, Donovan."

"Thanks," I said in somebody else's voice as he abandoned me to my fate.

The first question appeared on the screen. I read it over—once, twice, three times. No idea. None. Zero. Zilch. *Nada*. Of course, I had known this was coming. But somehow you always hold out hope. Nobody was perfect. Maybe they'd give me the wrong test—like for second grade remedial. It was possible.

But, no. This was the real thing. And as I looked into those words and numbers and symbols that meant absolutely nothing to me, I could almost see Dr. Schultz waiting at the front door of Hardcastle Middle School. It wouldn't take long for him to find me there.

I felt the icy water that had surrounded James Donovan in 1912, and the suction of the sinking *Titanic* pulling him under. James had resisted, but I didn't have the strength. I was going down.

There was one final chance. The test was multiple choice. I had a one-in-five shot at being right. It wasn't much, but at least it was something.

I took hold of the mouse to make my first fatal selection. And then something strange happened. As I moved the pointer toward box B, the small arrow changed direction and traveled on its own to check box C.

I stared, thunderstruck. Was there a problem with

the computer? Just my luck! On top of all the things that were stacked up against me, I was taking the test at a broken workstation. Although, come to think of it, I was just as capable of getting the wrong answers on my own, without any help from a malfunction. I considered changing C to B. But C was just as likely to be correct. So I left it, and clicked *Next*.

Question 2 seemed to have something to do with chemistry. But again, way out of my league. This time I settled on A, because—well, did there have to be a reason? I clicked it, and then it happened again. I lost control of the pointer. It deselected my choice, and immediately checked box E.

Then, without any action from me, it hit *Next,* and question 3 appeared.

Maybe I wasn't gifted, but I had the brains to know that this was no electronic glitch. There could be only one possible explanation for it. My computer had been hacked! Somebody was taking the test for me!

My first reaction was an emotional one. Another human being cared enough to want to keep me at the Academy! Most of my classmates were so wrapped up in their own skills and talents that they barely noticed anybody else existed. Yet someone had noticed me, and this person was going to great lengths, and risking big trouble, to bail me out.

For a second there, my eyes actually filled with tears, and I almost missed my remote angel answering question 3. I would have bet money that I had no friends in this place. But somewhere in this building—or even outside of it—hunched over a laptop, was the greatest friend I never knew I had. Would the Daniels do something like this for me? Okay, the Daniels couldn't pass this test if an alien microcomputer crash-landed inside their skulls. But even if they could, would they go out on a limb for me? I sincerely doubted it.

Who was doing it? They were all smart enough, but it took more than smarts. It took guts, and that was in short supply at the Academy. It could even be a teacher—Oz or Bevelaqua, trying to prove that the gifted program didn't make mistakes.

I noticed the librarian looking at me curiously, so I took hold of the mouse, and pretended to be busy at work. By that time, "I" was on question 11, and cruising. My bewilderment was beginning to morph into relief. My date with Dr. Schultz, and the consequences of the Atlas incident, had been put on hold. I was dogpaddling again. This time it took a little help—okay, a lot of help. But I was still afloat, just like James Donovan.

The librarian shot me an encouraging smile. What she saw was a student who had all the answers.

And I did. Except one.

Who was doing this for me?

# UNFORGIVABLE

## MS. BEVELAQUA
## IQ: 140

It makes perfect sense that a class with a teacher named Oz would call their robot Tin Man. The parallel to *The Wizard of Oz* doesn't stop there. In the famous story, the Tin Man lacks a brain; what he gets instead is a diploma.

I'm beginning to suspect that's what happened with Donovan Curtis.

He passed the test with flying colors. It was wonderful. We were all really happy for him. Except that it meant exactly as much as the words printed on the Tin Man's parchment. He was still failing my class quite spectacularly. In science, his average was below 50 percent and below 40 in the chemistry and physics portions. He was passing English, but just barely. His C-minus in social studies was the jewel in his crown, except for robotics. He was running a B average there, but only because he was handy with a joystick—a mark of someone who has taken on a life of solemn worship at the altar of Xbox or PlayStation.

Does this sound like Academy material to you?

"He passed the test, Maria," Brian Del Rio, our principal, reminded me. "What more can we ask of him?"

"A decent grade would be nice," I retorted. "Or some faint trace that might indicate mastery of a subject."

"We cut Noah Youkilis a lot of slack," Brian challenged her. "Why shouldn't Donovan deserve the same consideration?"

I sighed. "You're comparing apples and oranges. Come to think of it, pumpkins and raisins." A more appropriate contrast might be Betelgeuse and the nucleus of a carbon atom. "Noah is the kind of mind that comes along once in a teaching career, if you're lucky."

"But the test—" the principal insisted.

"If I buy a dog, but when I open the carrier I find a hamster inside, is it a dog because that's what it says on the bill of sale? My powers of observation and reasoning trump words on a piece of paper. I don't know how he passed the test. I only know that he couldn't have."

Brian was adamant. He ran this place by the book. Donovan had passed and he was in. Everybody was covered—especially the principal. If there was blame to be assigned somewhere down the line, none of it was going to fall on him.

And it had to be in Brian's mind that Donovan had solved the Human Growth and Development problem by providing his pregnant sister as a lab rat. Now, there was an oversight that would have resounded with the parents. I couldn't fault him for being grateful for a solution. Parents can get ugly; parents of the gifted can be positively militant. What I *did* fault him for was allowing that gratitude to blind him to the truth about Donovan. Perhaps he thought it was harmless to harbor a mediocre student in the Academy. But that student was diluting the standards of the gifted program for everybody. Not to mention that Donovan was learning absolutely nothing here. He was entitled to a real education at his own level.

My colleagues seemed to be taking their lead from Brian. If the principal wasn't worried, what concern was it of theirs? Of course they knew that Donovan wasn't exactly acing their classes. But, hey, he'd passed the test. The test! It was as if they believed the test was an infallible superbeing that had descended to earth on a great space ark surrounded by thunderbolts of perfection.

Oz was the last bastion of sanity left in the building. He'd known from the beginning that something wasn't right about Donovan. He was the one who'd asked for the retest. Surely he wasn't complacent enough to put aside his teacher's instinct just because of a test score.

When I barged into the robotics lab, at first I thought it was deserted because the lights were out, and I couldn't see any people.

Then I looked down. There they all were—including Oz—lying flat on the floor with Katie Patterson, their pregnant lab rat. Loud, gasping, wheezing breaths issued from every throat.

"What's going on here?" I exclaimed, shocked, scanning the room for a chemical leak.

"We're breathing," Oz panted.

"I can hear that. Why can't you do it standing up with the lights on?"

"It's a new variation on Lamaze," Chloe explained. "Noah developed it. It's much better than the original."

And would you believe that my colleague made me wait until the end of the class before he managed to find time for me? I stood in the hall, fuming, listening to the scuba-respiration sounds coming from inside the lab. It took a while to resuscitate Noah, who had passed out from his own breathing technique. They were all red-faced and panting as they filed past me, but they looked vaguely pleased with themselves, as if they were accomplishing something. Maybe they were. Very little was beyond Noah's capabilities when he wasn't mounting a concerted effort to flunk.

I noted that they were grateful to their lab rat— but most of that gratitude was heaped on Donovan himself. And it wasn't only gratitude. It was genuine affection. Noah regarded him with nothing less than worship. Chloe cast him soulful glances that might have indicated a crush. Even Abigail seemed to have softened her attitude toward him.

Oz was practically glowing with triumph, mopping at his face with a paper towel. "I have to admit I had my doubts about this project," he said after his students had moved on. "But we've taken a course that was ninety percent giggling at the names of body parts and made it meaningful, and beautiful, and rooted in the real world! I'm going to write an article for *American Teacher*."

That would be a must-read—all about how every class should adopt its own pregnant woman. "We need to talk about Donovan."

He nodded. "Where would we be without him?"

"I'm not talking about Baby 101, Oz. I'm talking about Donovan as an Academy student. Have you noticed any improvement in his performance?"

"Oh, sure, he . . ." His voice trailed off.

"I didn't think so," I said crisply. "He's bailed you out on Human Growth and Development and he's the Mario Andretti of the robot-driving circuit. But his academics are no better than they ever were."

"Well then, how did he pass the test?" Oz demanded with growing defiance.

"Maybe he didn't," I mused, voicing for the first time a thought that had been nagging at me over the past few days.

"Are you saying he cheated?" he sputtered. "Impossible! He took that test over a secure internet connection directly from the state department of education. He was alone in the library with a staff member's eye on him every second."

"It's impossible for Donovan," I agreed. "But what about the others?"

His incredulous expression slowly settled into one of alarm. Of course the others were capable of hacking into a secure connection, some of them without breaking a sweat.

"Why would they do it?" he managed at last. "Why help him pass?"

"Open your eyes, Oz. They *love* him. And it isn't just because of his sister and the way he drives the robot. He's normal, he's casual, he's capable of having a good time. He's everything they can't seem to master, despite all their brains."

He looked melancholy. "I like him, Maria. Maybe he doesn't belong, but he's good for these kids. He completes them."

"He turned one of them into a cheater," I reminded him.

"Hey, we have no evidence of that."

And that was the whole problem. If one of Oz's superachievers had found an undetectable way to take control of a secure computer and do the test for Donovan, who would ever be smart enough to prove it?

# CHEATING INVESTIGATION
## INTERVIEW WITH DONOVAN CURTIS

**MS. BEVELAQUA:** Your score on the retest was remarkable, Donovan.

**DONOVAN:** Thanks.

**MS. BEVELAQUA:** It far outstrips any work that you've done in class. How do you explain that?

**DONOVAN:** I studied really hard.

**MS. BEVELAQUA:** Come, now. You know this isn't the kind of test you can study for.

**DONOVAN:** Maybe I got lucky. Some people are just good test takers.

**MS. BEVELAQUA:** Or maybe someone helped you.

**DONOVAN:** I was all alone. Ask the librarian.

**MS. BEVELAQUA:** It's possible to take control of a computer remotely. In that case, someone would be able to do the test for you.

**DONOVAN:** I wouldn't have a clue how to do that.

**MS. BEVELAQUA:** I believe you. In fact, you've just proved my point. You could never accomplish such a thing. But the person who achieved that score could.

**DONOVAN:** I don't know what you're talking about.

**MS. BEVELAQUA:** Yes, you do. I want the name, and I want it now.

**DONOVAN:** I'm late for robotics.

**MS. BEVELAQUA:** You realize that we're talking about cheating here.

**DONOVAN:** You know the kind of kids in my class. Who'd risk that kind of trouble to help someone like me?

**MS. BEVELAQUA:** Perhaps nobody. But to help the brother of a living, breathing Human Growth and Development credit . . .

# UNREAL

## KATIE PATTERSON
### IQ: 107

**W**ell, it was official, confirmed by the vet. Beatrice wasn't dying. She wasn't even some evil demon dog dumped into the world for the purpose of ruining my life. She had a reason for her nasty behavior. The chow chow was as pregnant as I was. I never thought I'd say this, but she had my sympathy.

And that was pretty pregnant. Dr. Orsini said Beatrice might even whelp before I did. That came out wrong. Beatrice was the one who would be whelping. *I* would be giving birth. And while I knew exactly who the father was, the jury was still out on Beatrice. Odds were, we were about to welcome a litter of serious mongrels. And if you've ever seen a chow chow, you'll know they don't mix well with any other breed. So the Westminster Kennel Club was out.

I still hadn't worked up the nerve to tell Brad—even though the whole fiasco was his mother's fault, not mine. To be honest, I didn't like to distract him with the kind of problems that would seem silly to someone fighting a war. Plus, he'd been emailing me about how relaxed and happy I seemed lately, and I didn't want to spoil it by dumping this big matzoh ball in his lap.

From: First Lieutenant H. Bradley Patterson, United States Marine Corps
Honey, you're the best! I know this has been a stressful time with me away and the baby coming. What's your secret? . . .

My secret?

Reality check—I felt like I'd swallowed an anvil and it was lodged behind my belly button. I'd gained thirty-two pounds. A stiff wind was enough to knock me off balance. I had to sit so far back from the dinner table, I needed a telescope to see my food. My legs were covered with varicose veins. My back ached. My skin had broken out, thanks to my raging hormones. I couldn't allow myself to be more than sixty feet from a bathroom. Yeah, I felt wonderful.

Was it the news that the dog wasn't dying? Ha! Just because Beatrice was okay didn't mean she wasn't driving me nuts. For the past month she'd had no appetite at all; now she was eating us out of house and home. She had no bladder control, so the carpet was a minefield. She was antisocial to everyone except Donovan. And her new hobby was disappearing. The last time she vanished it took an hour to find her curled up inside a bale of pink insulation in the furnace room, and longer than that to pick the fiberglass fragments out of her coat.

I'd moved back in with my parents and kid brother, a world away from my husband, who was fighting in a war zone. My life stunk, no doubt about it.

But Brad was right. He had read between the lines of my emails. I *was* relaxed, even happy. Positively serene.

Why?

It had to be Human Growth and Development. For

some reason it was like therapy. Only instead of telling my innermost secrets to some high-priced shrink, I was spilling my guts to Donnie's geek patrol. For free!

Trust me, I could have killed my brother when he blackmailed me into serving as their class pet like a lizard in a glass terrarium. It would have been uncomfortable enough in front of normal kids. But to be stared at by these geniuses with their Coke-bottle glasses and analytical frowns—it was like being dissected and having your vital organs spread out on slides. At first, I had to pretend I was floating above my body, and that was somebody else down there being studied.

But then there was this one morning when I got out of bed and stepped right into one of Beatrice's puddles. By the time I got that sopped up, my spine felt like the disc spaces were filled with lava, but my mother only wanted to talk about the wonky pilot light in the furnace. So I wrote an email to Brad that was so full of whining and complaining, you could have set it to music. I deleted it without sending. Reality check— the poor man was risking his life every day. He didn't need to hear my problems.

That was when I glanced at my watch and realized that I was counting the minutes until I could go to the Academy and lay out my complaints to the only people who seemed to be interested. Chloe, Abigail, Latrell, Jacey, Kevin, even Noah—they'd understand because they understood *everything*. They knew more about me than my husband; they knew more about my pregnancy than my doctor—and they were a lot easier to reach than either of them.

When friends took me out to dinner, and I was unsure whether or not it was safe to eat oysters, I texted Chloe. I had the answer I needed—cooked, okay; raw, never—within thirty seconds. When I noticed an odd chemical on the ingredient list of my shampoo, I emailed Abigail, who was able to tell me it was just a harmless preservative. When I became alarmed by a strange rash on my belly, I had the perfect resource to turn to. I watched Noah's YouTube video "Stomach of Champions," which proved that the skin had been like that for weeks.

How had I survived without those guys?

Until Human Growth and Development I hadn't realized how *alone* I was, even among my own family. Going to those medical appointments was like walking the Tour de France route, up steep hills and over broken roads, all by myself. But when I saw the minibus parked outside the clinic, my spirits soared because

I knew I had a team with me—even if it was a robotics team. One day, the bus broke down on the way to the office. Dr. Manolo wouldn't start the appointment until the kids had arrived. He forwarded Oz Listserv emails from the American Congress of Obstetricians and Gynecologists. This class wasn't just going to pass Human Growth and Development. They were going to be qualified to teach it. All except Donnie. If there was one of them who didn't have a clue, it was my lunkhead brother.

What was he doing with these brilliant, motivated students? That was the biggest reality check of them all. Was it that, as his sister, I couldn't see how gifted he really was? Or did he just not care about this course because he already had the credit?

We were replaying the results of my fetal echocardiogram, watching the image of my baby's tiny heart beating on the Smart Board. It was entrancing. Chloe was almost in tears at the beauty of it. Abigail scribbled pages of notes, all without looking away from the screen. Noah had the flip cam trained on the monitor, so I knew this would be on YouTube in Kandahar before I got home that day to warn Brad that it was coming. The whole class, including the teacher, was fascinated.

All but Donnie. He was bored out of his mind, struggling to keep his butt in his chair. And he lost the struggle, jumping up and mumbling, "Going to the bathroom." He practically galloped out of the room.

A few minutes later, a couple of visitors walked into the lab, and Oz paused the video. I knew one was the principal, Mr. Del Rio. The other looked like a congressman, or some other kind of big shot, an older guy in a very snazzy suit.

He walked right up to me, smiled warmly, and held out his hand. "I'm Dr. Schultz, superintendent of the Hardcastle schools. I came specifically to meet you, Mrs. Patterson, and thank you for what you're doing for this class."

*That's* why he looked familiar. He used to be the principal at North High when I was a cheerleader at Hardcastle. He's the jerk who lodged a complaint that our uniforms were too "minimalist." He'd been a stuffed shirt back then, and it didn't seem as if that had changed now that he had the top job.

But all that was in the past, especially my cheerleading career. I was a mature adult, almost a mother. I shook his hand. "I'm happy to do it. They're great kids."

Dr. Schultz went on for a while—how selfless I was,

people should follow my example, my brother was so grateful, blah, blah, blah. He seemed to think that a) Donnie needed the credit I was providing, and b) Donnie was actually *here*, and not in the bathroom. Neither Oz nor Mr. Del Rio corrected him, though. I guess you don't interrupt a superintendent, even when he hasn't got his facts straight.

Then Donnie made his return—at least he started to. His head poked in through the doorway. His eyes widened in horror at the sight of Dr. Schultz—like I was standing with Count Dracula, not the superintendent of schools. Donnie backed up and was gone in a heartbeat. No one else noticed him. For sure Schultz didn't.

I don't claim to be an expert, but I knew my brother. He was scared to death of the guy. Something was up.

The class went on to show Dr. Schultz some of the work we'd been doing. He seemed impressed by the echocardiogram and the sonogram footage, but he didn't have much patience for Noah's new breathing technique. The superintendent had begun glancing impatiently at his watch.

Noah wasn't offended. "That's okay. You can watch it on my personal YouTube channel, Youkilicious."

"Let us introduce you to Tin Man at least," Oz

offered. He looked around for his designated driver. "Where's Donovan? Not on another one of his extended bathroom breaks?"

"Some other time," Dr. Schultz said briskly. He turned to me. "Thank you once again, Mrs. Patterson. You're a credit to the Hardcastle community." And he and the principal slipped out of the lab.

I waited a few minutes and then took a bathroom break of my own. Once in the hall, I headed straight for the boys' room, figuring my brother would be holed up there.

I threw open the door and broadcast a warning. "Big stomach waddling in."

"There's nobody here but us toilet paper" was the timid reply.

"You can come out now, Donnie. The guy's gone."

He emerged from a stall, wearing a guilty look that I'd seen a million times before.

I folded my arms, resting them on the shelf that my stomach now formed. "All right, out with it."

He looked haunted. "You don't want to know."

"Of course I don't want to know. But I think I have to."

Not even growing up in the same house with Donnie could have prepared me for the story I heard next.

Donnie—the Atlas statue—the Hardcastle gym. As reality checks go, this one had me pinching myself to see if I was hallucinating. It wasn't impossible, you know. On rare occasions, the chemical changes of pregnancy have been known to bring on psychotic episodes. I got that from Noah himself.

I heaved a sigh. "And you had the nerve to blackmail me over something as insignificant as a sick dog who wasn't even sick. That's low."

He shrugged miserably. "I'm sorry, but I'm trying to make myself a part of this class. They need you, so they're stuck with me, regardless of how ungifted I am."

"Your teachers are going to notice that you don't measure up," I pointed out gently.

"They already noticed. They had me retested. I passed."

"No way!"

He reddened. "Well, it wasn't really me. Somebody hacked into the computer I was using and did the test for me. Honest, I had nothing to do with it! I don't even know who it was."

I groaned. "That's worse. You've taken one of those brilliant students and corrupted him. Or her." I thought of Chloe, who seemed to be my brother's biggest fan.

"Well, what choice did I have?" he demanded, practically whining. "Bevelaqua already raked me over the coals, trying to get me to confess!"

"Did you ever consider going to Dr. Schultz and owning up?"

He was outraged. "Oh, sure! And Mom and Dad will collect soda bottles to get the money to fix the gym!"

I was astounded. "Who said we'd have to pay?"

"Come on, Katie. I may not be gifted, but I read the papers. The district is getting stiffed by the insurance company. Somebody has to pick up the tab—why not the guy who did it? I can't lay all that on Mom and Dad—not with money so tight, and Brad out of the picture, and you moping around, big as a whale. Even the dog went and made more problems. This is the worst possible time for me to add to all that."

I was thunderstruck, staring at my idiot brother with a new respect. This was the first indication I'd ever had that Donnie was aware of anybody besides himself. It jarred me down to my swollen ankles.

"Give me some time to mull this over," I told him. "I'd like to get Brad's opinion. Maybe he'll have an idea how we can explain all this to Dr. Schultz."

"Tell him to come quick," Donnie advised. "And bring his tank."

And right there, in the bathroom where *I* didn't belong, in the Academy where *he* didn't belong, the two of us shared a brother–sister hug.

Reality check—Dad kept a picture on his desk of the last time *that* happened—Disney World, 2002. I was sixteen. Donnie was three.

# UNMASKED

## DR. SCHULTZ
## IQ: 127

I was in my car heading back to the office, but something didn't sit well with me. I couldn't quite put my finger on it. Expressing my appreciation to Mrs. Patterson had been the right thing to do. We all had dodged a bullet, thanks to her. She had saved the district an enormous amount of aggravation. Irate parents; frantic phone calls; summer plans changed; complaints to the school board and maybe even the state. It would have been the biggest screwup of the year—well, second biggest.

Perhaps it was the Academy itself that had unnerved me. That place always made me uneasy. Don't get me wrong—gifted programs are an essential resource for a school district. The trouble with them is they attract so many know-it-alls!

I stopped at a light, frowning. Something Kyle Osborne had said was still rattling around my head: "Where's"—I couldn't recall the name; Dominic? Donnelly?—followed by: "Not on another one of his extended bathroom breaks?"

Extended bathroom breaks . . .

That was the answer. It was common enough for an unmotivated student to kill time in the bathroom, hoping to make the days speed by. But not at the Academy. There were no mediocre students there. And if one of our best and brightest had decided to squander his placement, he should step aside in favor of someone who wouldn't waste the opportunity.

As soon as I was back at my desk, I called Brian Del Rio. Maybe he could identify this missing kid.

He was out of the office. "Page him, please," I said, and sat back to wait.

As my eyes passed over the screen saver on my computer, it occurred to me that Brian might not be my only source of information about that class. There was also Noah's YouTube channel—I winced—Youkilicious.

Not the easiest name to spell, but I found it soon enough and stared in amazement: 114 featured videos? Noah had the highest IQ in the history of the district, but from the looks of this, all the boy did was run around with a flip camera!

My attention was instantly drawn to "Tin Man Metallica Squarepants Exposes Teacher's Underwear." God bless America, it had already been viewed more than six thousand times! That wasn't good. What could be a bigger screwup than a lawsuit over the misconduct of a robot?

I clicked on the link and the clip began to play. It showed Maria Bevelaqua laying papers on a semicircle of desks. As she moved, Tin Man rolled into the picture, falling in behind her, matching her pace almost perfectly. The forklift mechanism began to rise, catching the hem of her full peasant skirt. Up it went, until there was more of Ms. Bevelaqua on the screen than I cared to see. Judging by the giggles in the background of the video, the last person to notice this was Maria herself. When she finally did, the screech prompted my computer to warn me that my speakers were in danger. And right before the clip ended, the camera swung around and focused on the student who was operating the robot's joystick controller.

My blood turned to ice in my veins.

It was—it was—

I had a vision of an upturned face staring wide-eyed into the wreckage of the Hardcastle gym. That nameless face was the first thing I saw every morning, and the last thing I saw at night. It had starred in my wildest nightmares, taunting me, driving me crazy for weeks.

Dominic . . . Donnelly . . . *Donovan.*

It was *him.*

# CHEATING INVESTIGATION
## INTERVIEW WITH CHLOE GARFINKLE

**MS. BEVELAQUA:** I've noticed that you and Donovan are pretty good friends.

**CHLOE:** I guess.

**MS. BEVELAQUA:** It would bother you if he had to leave the Academy, wouldn't it?

**CHLOE:** Why would he have to leave?

**MS. BEVELAQUA:** You have a brilliant mind, Chloe. You must have noticed that Donovan doesn't share your academic abilities.

**CHLOE:** He's good at a lot of things I'm not.

**MS. BEVELAQUA:** You know as well as I do that operating a video game joystick doesn't compare to the kinds of strengths we value here.

**CHLOE:** Well, maybe. But he passed the test.

**MS. BEVELAQUA:** Did he?

**CHLOE:** You'd know better than I would. The scores were reported to the school, not to me.

**MS. BEVELAQUA:** We're beginning to suspect that someone helped Donovan. Was it you, Chloe?

**CHLOE:** How could I possibly—you mean a hacker?

That would be hard. You'd have to override the encryption of a secure internet connection from the state!

**MS. BEVELAQUA:** Exactly. I see you know how it's done.

**CHLOE:** Yeah, but that doesn't mean I'd do it! Not for my own mother!

**MS. BEVELAQUA:** But for your boyfriend?

**CHLOE:** Donovan is not my boyfriend! I don't have a boyfriend!

**MS. BEVELAQUA:** Calm down. No one is making any accusations—yet.

**CHLOE:** Honestly, Ms. Bevelaqua, we knew Donovan was in trouble with the test. We offered to help him study, but he just couldn't—it didn't work out.

**MS. BEVELAQUA:** Define "we." You and who else?

**CHLOE:** Are you asking me to rat out my friends?

# UNWELCOME
## DONOVAN CURTIS
### IQ: 112

was pretty good at video games, but never had I felt more comfortable with a joystick in my hand than when I was driving Tin Man. The robot was like an extension of my will. The slightest twitch of my finger and he was instantly obedient to the controller. It was as if my every thought could make him dance.

For once, we weren't in the lab. With the state robotics meet barely a week away, it was time to simulate competition conditions. The team had spent all morning converting the gym into a perfect copy of the Dutchess Auditorium, where the tournament would take place. Tin Man moved back and forth, accepting inflated rings from Abigail and placing them on the pegs we had attached to the gym's climbing apparatus. We'd even set up the "pit," which would serve as our headquarters at the meet. It supplied everything from tools and spare parts for Tin Man to a cooler of "YoukilAde"—a high-energy drink that, according to Noah, hydrated faster than Gatorade.

Most of the team was gathered around Oz, their eyes panning back and forth from the robot to the teacher's stopwatch. They let out an audible groan when I raised one of the rings too high, and had to stop the robot to lower the mechanism down to the peg. That cost us time for sure.

"Easy, Donovan," the teacher cautioned. "Remember, you've got a stronger motor in the forklift."

At last, Tin Man placed the final ring, swung around, and headed for the starting position. The stopwatch beeped and Oz called out our time. "Best we've ever done, people. Even with a few hiccups."

"This is going to be our year!" Latrell crowed.

We broke out the YoukilAde and toasted Tin Man and one another. Chloe had brought brownies, so it was kind of a party. It actually reached the point of some good-natured trash talk directed toward Cold Spring Harbor, and how Tin Man was going to leave their robot lying in the dust.

Of course, our team members were too polite for *real* trash talk, so I had to show them how it was done: "Their hunk of junk doesn't stand a chance against Tin Man! Their hunk of junk wouldn't stand a chance against Tin Man's *grandmother*!"

"Tin Man can't have a grandmother," Noah interjected. "A machine is not a living entity, and has no familial line."

Probably why I never ran into any robots on ancestry.com.

"We get the point," Oz put in, grinning. "Let's keep it to ourselves. It's a little premature for a victory celebration."

"There's no way Cold Spring Harbor can match the kind of times we're putting up," Kevin enthused. "Not unless they're running their robot on rocket fuel."

I'd never been much of a joiner, so this was my first taste of how it felt to be part of a team that was a real contender. And not just a part. With the robot completed, I was more important than any of them. All those geniuses, and the one person who could make Tin Man perform at championship level was the dummy who got stranded in the gifted program by mistake. I didn't have a clue how to design, build, or program a robot. But it was up to me to bring home the gold.

For the first time since I'd landed at the Academy, I truly *belonged*.

The heavy metal gym door was thrown open with such violence that it pounded against the cinder block wall. There, framed in the light from outside, was nothing less than an avenging angel.

Dr. Schultz.

I swear he crossed the gym in three gigantic strides, shooting sparks from his eyes. I considered running, but what for? Even if I could manage to escape, where did I think I could go? I was completely and totally busted.

"Dr. Schultz—what a surprise," said Oz. "You're just in time to see us put Tin Man through his paces."

"That will have to happen some other time." The superintendent's voice was colder than his expression, if possible. The eyes fell on me. "Donovan Curtis— your parents are on their way."

Chloe was the first to clue in to the gravity of what was going on. "Donovan might not be gifted in the same way as the rest of us, but he's the heart and soul of our team! He's the heart and soul of our *class*!"

Dr. Schultz regarded her sternly. "Donovan's problems go far beyond trying to be what he's not."

I followed him out of the gym, while the squawking and protesting of my teammates rang off the rafters.

"He drives the robot!"

"We're dead without him!"

"He is *so* gifted!"

"He brought us Katie!"

"He showed me YouTube!"

"He's one of us!"

Their support would have made me feel good if I hadn't been on my way to the end of the world.

I scrubbed hard with the polishing cloth, and Madagascar got a little shinier. Maybe. It was so dark in the subbasement of the administration building that it was hard to tell Africa from South America.

I was in the dungeon—or at least the closest thing they had to a dungeon in the Hardcastle school district. My sentence was to polish up the bronze world I had knocked off Atlas's shoulders all those weeks ago. The worst part wasn't the polishing; it was chipping off years of bird droppings that had ossified by a chemical process I'll bet even Noah Youkilis couldn't explain.

It was all useless, of course. There was no way Schultz was going to put this thing up again. Not after what had happened. But he wanted it perfect and gleaming in its hiding place. Actually, what he really wanted was for me to suffer. Believe it or not, cleaning the celestial sphere—as part of twenty hours of community service—was my only punishment for everything that had happened. My family was not going to have to pay for repairs to the Hardcastle gym. I was off the hook—a survivor, just like my ancestor, James Donovan, when he climbed out of the icy North Atlantic and into the lifeboat. Whacking the statue with a branch had been a dumb thing to do, but, in the end, it fell within the range of normal wear and tear. The rusted bolt was at fault, not me. Now the only question was, would the insurance company pay for a design flaw from a foundry that no longer existed?

"You got off easy, Donovan Curtis," the superintendent had told me sternly at the meeting with my parents. "I hope you realize that this could have gone a lot harder on you."

He called me by my full name, almost as if he was afraid he might forget it again. I couldn't blame him. These past weeks must have been like chasing a ghost.

That's probably why he was so animated when he added, "I suppose I don't have to tell you that you're no longer a student at the Academy for Scholastic Distinction."

Seated between Mom and Dad, I'd recoiled as if he'd slapped me. I didn't much care about the Academy— I'd never belonged there in the first place. But it hurt to be off the robotics team.

My mother cried, but that wasn't exactly breaking news. She cried whenever anyone got voted off the island on reality TV. I understood her disappointment. As of today, I wasn't gifted anymore. Not only that, but I was responsible for the biggest town disaster since the famous gas-line explosion of 1986, which ruptured a drainage pipe and filled the Hardcastle Public Library with raw sewage up to the second floor.

Worse still was how Dad took it in stride. Some of that might have been his good mood at finding out he wasn't going to have to foot the bill for a new gym. Mostly, though, it said he had never truly believed I was gifted in the first place.

His only comment was, "Do you think turpentine will take that bumper sticker off the car?"

I never gave much thought to the fact that me being

at the Academy had been such a big deal to him. But for some reason, it bugged me that he wasn't more upset to learn that the whole thing was a sham.

"You always suspected, huh, Dad?"

He was quiet for a moment, then, "You know that website you like—the one about the ancestors and great-granduncles and old-time relatives? Well, I did my share of that kind of poking around when I was your age."

That didn't make sense. "They had ancestry.com when you were a kid?"

"Well, back then they called it the library. But if you go through enough microfiches, you can learn the same things. The names you dig up, I've heard most of them before—Irish forebears who moved to America, Canada, England, Australia—places like that."

Amazing! I still couldn't explain why I did the things I did. But at least now I understood why I turned to ancestry.com to look for answers.

"All those people went on to different jobs," he continued. "Teacher, construction worker, lawyer, grave digger—even a mayor and a couple of city councilmen. As far as I can tell, they all lived satisfying, happy, productive lives, but you know what? Not one of them was especially gifted. Think about that, and maybe you'll see why I'm not so crushed about this. What matters—the only part I really care about—is that you're happy."

It was an impressive speech for a normally quiet guy like my dad. There was only one problem: I *wasn't* happy. In fact, I was pretty far from it.

It was completely outside my control, but I felt like I was letting the robotics team down. For sure Tin Man wasn't going to win anything with Abigail at the joystick. Worse, Katie was quitting Human Growth and Development.

"If they boot my brother, they boot me too," she said stoutly. "Who says you're not gifted?"

"*You* do," I replied honestly. "And it's the truth. Come on, Katie, it wasn't the kids who kicked me out. They're still fourteen hours short for their credit. They'll have to go to summer school!"

"That's tough!" she snapped. "Summer school will be good for them. Let them see how the other half lives!"

What could I say? She was supporting me. Strange she should choose to start now. I felt bad, but I had to let it go. Dr. Schultz had spelled it out. That place wasn't my life anymore. In the real world, it never had been.

\* \* \*

My locker was gone. I mean, it was still there. But while I was at the Academy, the administration had hacksawed my lock off, and all my stuff had vanished. At the office, they told me to make a list of the missing items. I tried, but the only thing worth more than three cents was one combination lock. So I gave up.

I kept seeing my locker at the Academy—spacious, freshly painted, its built-in power strip waiting to help me by keeping my devices charged—not that I had any devices. By comparison, my Hardcastle locker was about the size of a tiny apartment mailbox. It smelled like feet.

The whole building was an extension of my locker—shabby, crumbling, depressing. The Academy was a palace by comparison. I don't know if I appreciated it when I was there, but I definitely appreciated it now, surrounded by broken drinking fountains and crumbling plaster. Week-old lunches overflowed out of every garbage can. The halls rang with the voice of an assistant principal, chewing out some poor kid over a random offense. Nobody took you for a cooling-off walk and a philosophical discussion at Hardcastle. Here, a paper airplane was not an experiment in aerodynamics. It was an act of war.

I tried to work up more gratitude for being off the hook for the Atlas incident. This place just crushed it out of me. I doubt James Donovan ever stood on the deck of the *Carpathia* and yearned to return to the icy water, but I couldn't stop itching for a rewind button to whoosh me back to the Academy. It was stupid, I know. I never said I was gifted. I just wish I'd been better at faking it.

The Daniels arranged a homecoming for me that I'm not soon going to forget. In front of the entire lunch crowd in the cafeteria, they presented me with the 2012 Moron of the Year Award, which looked suspiciously like the missing toilet from the upstairs boys' room. On the bowl, in dribbling red paint, was written: WELCOME HOME, STUPID. It weighed a ton and a half.

"Here he is, back from a very limited engagement at the Academy for Scholastic Dork-stinction, the man who turned out to be just as lamebrained as the rest of us—give it up for *Donovan 'The Dummy' Curtis!*"

I didn't die of humiliation. I only wanted to. There were a few lukewarm cheers, but most of the kids didn't know quite what to make of it. I'd only been gone a few weeks. Half of them might have figured I took a long trip, or had mono, or got suspended or something. Probably a lot of them thought: Who's Donovan Curtis?

"Come on, you guys!" Sanderson goaded the crowd. "If it isn't loud, he won't understand it!"

I hefted my "award"—which must have tipped the scale at thirty-five pounds—and swung it at the Daniels. The seat came off, whacking Nussbaum in the back of the head before cracking on the floor. That got a bigger response than the announcement of my award. My one consolation was that Chloe wasn't here to witness this. I didn't know for sure, but she struck me as a pacifist. At any rate, toilet fighting was probably a no-no. This might have cured her of her longing to be "normal." If it didn't, she was nuts.

"Come on, man," Nussbaum offered. "We'll buy you lunch."

"I brought my lunch," I said stubbornly. .

"Then grab a table," Sanderson instructed, rubbing the back of his head. "And don't forget your award—what's left of it."

I was wary. "I'm not going to get blamed for stealing this, am I? I'm running low on schools I haven't been kicked out of yet."

"See, that's what's been missing around here," Nussbaum noted. "That Donovan sense of humor.

Welcome home, bro. The place wasn't the same without you."

We had lunch with Heather and Deirdre. Apparently, those four had been eating together for weeks. That made me the party crasher. I'd thought the one good thing about coming back to Hardcastle was at least I'd fit in. Guess again.

As it turned out, I had to throw my sandwich away. It had spent the morning in my locker, and now the mayonnaise tasted like feet. I took handouts from my four companions.

Girls put avocado in everything.

I was back with friends, or what passed for that. Funny—I'd been convinced I was friendless at the Academy. But I'd felt more a part of things in Oz's robotics lab than anywhere here at Hardcastle. How could I compare the Daniels and their jokey, in-your-face version of friendship to the guardian angel/hacker who had risked everything to pass that test for me? Now, with the Academy permanently in my rearview mirror, I still had no idea who it was. I would have liked to say thank you. In a weird way, though, that person was even more ungifted than me. It made no sense to believe that a test score could make me into something I wasn't.

Classes at my new old school weren't better, exactly, but at least I understood what was going on. I'd been faking it for so long at the Academy that it was startling to suddenly know actual answers. I even raised my hand a few times in math, until Sanderson bounced a spitball off my skull and hissed, "Dude—this isn't the Academy!"

And I couldn't help thinking, No, it sure isn't. You can see it in the paint job, and taste it in the bad cafeteria food. You can hear it in the dead air that hangs in the classroom when the teacher asks a question. You can smell it in the sweaty gym socks—so different from the synthetic-oil aroma of a set of Mecanum wheels.

While I was in the bathroom, someone stole my toilet—the award one, not the one I was using.

I made a mental note to buy Febreze for my locker.

On the way home, the Daniels and I passed by the statue of Atlas. I hadn't been there for a while, not wanting to revisit the scene of the crime. The titan was still oddly bent, with no celestial sphere to weigh him down. And, at the bottom of the hill, the entrance to the high school gym remained boarded shut. I'd been so wrapped up in my own weird predicament that I hadn't given much thought to the mess I'd made over here. The wave of remorse was stronger than I'd anticipated. Suddenly, twenty hours of scraping pigeon poop off a bronze sphere seemed like no more than I deserved.

"You've done a lot of crazy stuff," Nussbaum sighed, "but this was your finest hour."

"It wasn't so fine for the gym," I said bitterly. "Or for me."

Sanderson nodded thoughtfully. "You're right. It would have been better if the globe had gone crashing into the parking lot. It could have smashed, like, ten, fifteen cars."

I glared at them. "You guys deserve the toilet award more than me."

Nussbaum grinned appreciatively. "Good to have you back where you belong."

*Where I belong.* I looked at the gray, dreary hulk of Hardcastle Middle School, and felt deeply bummed that he was probably right.

# CHEATING INVESTIGATION
## INTERVIEW WITH ABIGAIL LEE

**MS. BEVELAQUA:** You're aware, of course, that Donovan Curtis has left the school for good.

**ABIGAIL:** He never should have been here. I knew that from the first day.

**MS. BEVELAQUA:** As did I. Which brings up the question of how he managed to pass the retest. We believe that someone took control of his computer, and helped him cheat. Was it you?

**ABIGAIL:** You must be joking! I'm the last person who would help that guy! His presence lowered Academy standards for every one of us. Why would I want to help him stay?

**MS. BEVELAQUA:** Well, for one thing, his sister was providing you with a Human Growth and Development credit. Then there's the robotics team, in which he had taken a key role.

**ABIGAIL:** Oh, please. He worked a joystick like any other half-witted gamer.

**MS. BEVELAQUA:** Except that a better driver could have meant the difference between winning and losing. It's been my observation that you're not too keen on losing.

**ABIGAIL:** Nobody likes to lose.

**MS. BEVELAQUA:** I know how you think, Abigail. For you, education is more than learning. It's a high-stakes chess match. The state robotics meet is a resumé builder. A better resumé means a better college. A better college means a better future. Just how far would you be willing to go to assure all that?

**ABIGAIL:** Part of strategy is risk *vs.* return. Why would I risk getting busted for cheating over a jerk I can't even stand?

# UNBELIEVABLE

## CHLOE GARFINKLE
## IQ: 159

<<*Hypothesis: Truth is stranger than fiction.*>>

**M**ake that *way* stranger.

At the Academy, we're taught to think outside the box. But to guess this, you'd have to be so far outside the box that you couldn't find your way back with a GPS.

The disaster at the Hardcastle gym—that was Donovan. And by some misunderstanding growing out of it, he'd been sent to the Academy and parachuted into our lives.

Abigail had been right, as usual. He didn't belong. She'd said it first, but since then, every one of us had at least thought it. He'd *never* belonged. There was not a single imaginable reason why Donovan Curtis should ever again set foot inside the Academy.

<<*Hypothesis: I don't care.*>>

"I miss him too, Chloe," Oz admitted when I finally cracked in front of him. "I think we all do. But there's no way he can ever come back."

"Why not?" I demanded.

"For starters, because it comes from Dr. Schultz himself, and his word is law in this district. And second, because there are dozens of requirements for admission into the Academy, and Donovan meets none of them. Besides, what would he do here?"

"What did he do when he *was* here?" I countered. "He brought us to life! He turned Tin Man from a nameless machine into a part of the family! We got a spirit from him that we don't have anymore! And next week we're going to sleepwalk into that robotics meet and finish dead last when we could have won it all! I don't know if I even want to go to this school anymore!"

He was horrified. "Chloe! You need the level of

academic challenge—"

"That academic challenge landed me in summer school!" I snapped. "And in case you forgot, Donovan had a solution for that too. And we threw him out."

"Katie had a choice," Oz argued. "She could have stayed with us and finished the course."

"Why would she, after the way we treated her brother? I don't blame her a bit. I blame us."

<<*Hypothesis: Desperate times call for desperate measures.*>>

I was so upset that I did something I'd never done before. I cut school that afternoon. Not just a class or two; all of it. I hopped on a crosstown bus, and rode east toward the one person who could help, if anybody could. I was going to Hardcastle Middle School to find Donovan.

The ride was endless, slow, stopping at every tiny un-street along the way. I kept checking the time on my phone, but it didn't move the bus any faster. I wasn't sure what the schedule was at Hardcastle, but dismissal had to be coming up pretty soon. To commit my first act of truancy in a spotless school career only to miss Donovan would be too much to bear.

I got off at the high school and started running up

the hill. There he was, Atlas, *sans* globe, overlooking the boarded-up gym. I took heart—this was definitely the right place. But my first sight of the middle school almost took my breath away. They were already coming out, swarming all over the campus, crowding onto buses.

I ran into the midst of the crowd, frantically scanning faces on the off chance I'd find the one I was searching for out of more than nine hundred. They all seemed familiar and unfamiliar at the same time. I'd probably seen many of them at the dance. But that didn't matter. Nobody was familiar *enough*.

I was beginning to get some strange looks. "Is Donovan Curtis around?" I asked one boy.

His response was a blank stare.

His companion shoved him. "The dude who dissed the basketball team."

"You know him?" I prompted.

"Not really."

<<*Hypothesis: Donovan made a bigger impression in just a few weeks at the Academy than in nearly three years here.*>>

I caught a glimmer of how someone could disappear among a student body of more than three hundred at each grade level. It could never happen at my school. You were famous for what you knew, or what you could do, or what you might become. Or, in Donovan's case, even for what you didn't know.

I tried another kid, a girl this time. "Do you know Donovan Curtis?"

She shrugged. "I heard he transferred to the Academy."

"I think he's back," piped up the boy behind her. "Isn't he the guy who won the toilet award?"

Probably. It sounded like him. "Have you seen him anywhere?"

Another shrug.

*<<Hypothesis: Non-Academy kids are very loose in the shoulders.>>*

I'd always envied them their relaxed casual attitude—something that never came naturally to us in the gifted program. But right now, I felt like I was drowning, and nobody cared enough to throw me a life preserver.

By this time, some of the school buses had taken off, and the crowd was thinning out. An ugly truth began weighing me down like a heavy meal. I wasn't going to find him. I'd come all this way for nothing. Worse,

I was going to have to get back on that crosstown bus and jounce my way home. I wasn't even really sure what I'd been planning to say to the guy. I just knew for certain that the mere sight of him would have settled me down.

Suddenly, a too-loud voice behind me announced, "Hey, isn't that the plaid chick?"

I wheeled. There they stood, staring at me, Donovan's two friends named Daniel. I ran over to them. "I'm so glad to see you guys—"

"Whoa—" One of them held out a hand. "Not too close! Your brain waves might fry my cell phone!"

"Guys, is Donovan still here?"

The taller Daniel sneered down at me. "Look who needs Donovan all of a sudden! You should have thought of that before you threw him out of your smarty-pants school!"

"Woulda, shoulda, coulda," put in the other one.

I ignored their baiting, and plowed forward. "I totally agree with you. If it was up to me, Donovan would still be at the Academy. That's what I came here to talk to him about. Has he left yet?"

"He wasn't in school today," the taller Daniel said finally. "Schultz took him to meet with the school district's insurance company. You know he's the guy who busted the gym, right?"

"We were eyewitnesses," added the other one. And he went into this ridiculous story about how Donovan had, for no reason at all, whacked the statue on the rump with a tree branch, and all the damage had happened because the globe had disconnected and rolled down the hill.

I was just about to say, "How stupid do you think I am?" when it dawned on me—that story was *totally* Donovan! It was exactly why he was so needed at the Academy. None of us ever did anything without thinking it out in detail, making an elaborate plan. Donovan *acted*—whether it was hitting a statue, or naming a robot, or stealing a motor, or finding someone to teach Human Growth and Development because she *was* Human Growth and Development. For Donovan, it was all as natural as breathing.

"Well," I stammered, "can you give me his phone number? I really need to talk to him."

Taller Daniel was indignant. "And give you brainiacs another chance to make him feel stupid? No way! He's miserable enough!"

And then, as if I hadn't sufficiently humiliated

myself, I began to sob like a heartbroken child. Part of it was pure frustration with this wild-goose chase—the fact that these two jerks could easily have put me in touch with Donovan, but they wouldn't. And part of it was this: I'd been so wrapped up in what *we'd* lost, how *we'd* suffered, the fact that *we'd* have to go to summer school; I'd never even wasted a thought on how Donovan must have felt about all this. How selfish was I?

<<*Hypothesis: We don't deserve Donovan at the Academy.*>>

"Hey, wait a minute!" the other Daniel exclaimed. "What are you doing?"

"Go ahead!" I sniffled. "Let me have it! Make fun of the Academy nerd crybaby! All I wanted to do was let him know how much we miss him, and how we've all been like zombies since he left! Next week is the robotics meet we've been preparing for all year, and now nobody even wants to go! I didn't come here to make him feel bad! I came to tell him how sorry we are!"

I fell silent, catching my breath, and waiting for them to laugh in my face. This was one more thing to regret for poor Donovan: He had such lousy friends.

The shorter Daniel took something out of his pocket

and began unfolding it meticulously. It was a T.G.I. Friday's napkin, crushed for who knows how long in a linty pocket. He handed it to me, and I blew my nose gratefully. Neither of them spoke. It was the first time I'd ever seen those guys at a loss for a snide remark.

Finally, the taller Daniel spoke up. "When did you say that robotics meet was?"

# CHEATING INVESTIGATION
## INTERVIEW WITH NOAH YOUKILIS

**MS. BEVELAQUA:** No, you may not film this interview. I've already made enough appearances on your YouTube channel. But we'll have that conversation on another day.

**NOAH:** We should reach ten thousand hits sometime next week. You know, based on the rate of increase of daily views. It's simple calculus—

**MS. BEVELAQUA:** I know that. I'm a math teacher. Please pay attention, Noah. Would it be possible for someone to take control of a computer that's transmitting over a secure internet connection?

**NOAH:** Oh, sure. You just have to create an application to decrypt the data. It's boring stuff.

**MS. BEVELAQUA:** And did you do it to make sure Donovan passed his retest?

**NOAH:** I thought of it, because we really need him around here. But it wouldn't have done any good, because he got kicked out anyway. You know that statue thing? That was Donovan. What a YouTube video that would have made . . .

**MS. BEVELAQUA:** Back up. You thought of it?

**NOAH:** Sure. I was going to do it. But I forgot.

**MS. BEVELAQUA:** And I'm supposed to believe that?

**NOAH:** I got busy shooting a video and, by the time I remembered, the test was over. Donovan was back in class, and he didn't seem upset, so I assumed he aced it. It is pretty easy, you know.

**MS. BEVELAQUA:** I can't believe you're being so casual about something this important. Cheating is a very grave offense, whether you do it for yourself or somebody else. You could get expelled from the Academy for that.

**NOAH:** Really?

# UNSCHOOLED

## DONOVAN CURTIS
### IQ: 112

According to ancestry.com, James Donovan went to Washington to testify as a witness at the Senate hearings into the sinking of the *Titanic*. That was what I had to do, only it was more like I was saying that I deliberately picked up the iceberg and sliced open the boat with it. According to Schultz, the insurance guys needed to hear the real story straight from the mouth of the person who did it. The executives looked like they were all going to go home and yell at their kids, just to keep them from turning out like me.

The worst part wasn't the testimony, but the one-on-one time with Schultz in his car. The guy hated me basically because *he* had made a mistake. Plus, he was such a slow driver that the trip took twice as long as it should have. And trust me, the conversation wasn't flowing. The only upside was, when he dropped me at home, Beatrice climbed into the car and peed on the floor mat. Believe it or not, I was starting to appreciate that dumb dog.

These days, the chow chow was kind of my soul mate around home. She moped; I moped. She hid in the basement and refused to talk to anybody; me too. We lay side by side on the furnace room floor, gazing up at the spots where the ductwork disappeared into the ceiling. Her belly was even more swollen than Katie's now. Sometimes you could actually see the skin rippling as the unborn puppies wriggled inside.

My mom tried to pretend she wasn't devastated by my new ungifted status. But I could read between the lines no matter what she said.

"I'm every bit as proud of you as I was the day before we got that letter." See the problem? Think about it. It'll come to you.

Katie was already nostalgic. "Strange but true, I miss

those geniuses. They're getting restless in Afghanistan. My stomach hasn't been on YouTube for a whole week."

My dad reported that the turpentine had worked, and he no longer was the proud parent of an honor student.

School was the worst. I couldn't hack it in the gifted program, but the work at Hardcastle was just too easy. Crazy as it seemed, all my fruitless studying at the Academy had stuck with me. Now I was getting straight A's—and instead of being happy about it, my good grades served as yet another reminder of the place I'd been kicked out of. It was like I had a foot in two different worlds, and they were moving apart. I was going to crack up the middle like a wishbone, and I didn't much care.

The Daniels kept trying to cheer me up. But their plans always involved doing something that would get me into trouble for their entertainment. One day they brought a stink bomb for me to set off in the cafeteria, and they were genuinely amazed when I said no. Believe me, it had nothing to do with following the rules. I just wasn't that guy anymore. I felt the presence of that bent-over Atlas, and I couldn't work up a stink-bombing mood.

It was the same with the vampire teeth for the skeleton in the science lab on Tuesday and the latex vomit for the teachers' dining room on Wednesday.

So when I got to school on Thursday, and saw the Daniels coming at me in the hall, I was wary. "What is it this time? Itching powder for the soap dispensers? Nerve gas for the ceiling fans? Cyanide for the salsa?"

"Better than that," Nussbaum promised. "You need a mental health day off from school."

"Be serious, you guys," I complained.

"Trust us," said Sanderson.

They wouldn't take no for an answer. I swear, I thought they were kidding, because they were always kidding. And besides, where could they possibly want to take me in the middle of a weekday, when it would be obvious to everyone that we were ditching?

They shoved me out the double doors at the side entrance. I was just about to fight my way back in when I recognized the car parked at the curb, waiting for us. The front seat was pushed all the way back to make room for the burgeoning stomach of the driver.

Katie.

"What's going on?" I demanded.

Nussbaum grinned. "Shut up and get in the car."

"Hey, Donnie." Katie greeted me as I got into the passenger seat and the Daniels crawled into the back. "Up for a road trip?"

I was mystified. "Where are we going?"

"Dude, it's a very special day," Sanderson reminded me, sitting forward until he was breathing down my neck.

"What day?"

"Well, let's work it out," Nussbaum pondered. "It's not my birthday, and it's not Cinco de Mayo. Christmas? No, that's already past. It's not the Fast of Gedalia, or Bastille Day—"

"Cut it out!" I snapped.

Katie was laughing. "Put him out of his misery. Tell him, already!"

"I can't believe you forgot," Sanderson scolded. "Your girlfriend is going to be really mad."

"What girlfriend?"

"You know—plaid Chloe with the big brain."

I bristled. "She's not my—" But the thought of Chloe made me remember. Today was the state robotics meet at the Dutchess Auditorium in St. Leo!

They were taking me to watch Tin Man.

My first thought was *I don't want to go.* Yet before the words made it out of my mouth, I realized that I *did* want to go. Possibly more than anything I'd ever wanted in my life. It would hurt to be sitting in the audience instead of in the pit with the joystick in my hand. But it was better than not being there at all. Tin Man was going into competition against Cold Spring Harbor and the top robots in the whole state. I should be there to cheer him on.

"I love a good robotics meet," Nussbaum enthused. "It's just like the Super Bowl, only nobody cares, and it's way more boring."

I shook my head. "How did you guys even know about this?"

"Don't look at me," Katie put in. "I'm just the driver. Your buddies put together the whole thing."

"Your girlfriend told us," Sanderson supplied. "She showed up looking for you, and she was all moaning and groaning, and a total downer pain in the butt. In other words, exactly like you've been lately. So we figured the only way to shut the two of you up was to get you together at a good old-fashioned robotics meet."

"Thanks—I think." But I didn't just think; I knew.

Who would have dreamed that there were real hearts hidden under all that baloney? Not even the gifted program could have predicted it.

St. Leo was forty-five miles from Hardcastle, but Katie needed two bathroom stops on the way, so it took more than an hour to get there. I was amazed at the size of the Dutchess Auditorium, which was a huge rambling building on the edge of town. The team had always said that the robotics meet was a big deal, but I guess I'd never really believed them.

"Maybe it *is* the Super Bowl," Nussbaum mused.

Inside, grandstands ringed the vast floor. On one side, a checkerboard of pits was laid out in an orderly fashion, providing home bases for the teams. I counted thirty-six of them. On the other side was the course, looking remarkably similar to what we'd laid out in the gym for Tin Man. Even though I wasn't a part of it anymore, I felt a jolt of excitement. My teammates had told me about this, had described it in such detail that I felt like I'd already seen it.

Katie, who had trouble standing for long periods of time, settled her awkward bulk into a seat, and reserved three more for the rest of us.

Sanderson leaned back in his chair and tipped the

peak of his baseball cap over his face. "If anything happens in the next four hours," he murmured, "wake me up."

"Are you kidding?" Nussbaum crowed. "It's like a nerd city down there! One good wedgie could start an epidemic!"

"Can it," I ordered. I had just spotted the Academy pit. I saw Latrell first, lying on his back, working on Tin Man's undercarriage. Tin Man! There were a lot of robots, but I only had eyes for ours. I hadn't built him, and I wouldn't be driving him, but the pride of ownership was electric.

"Hey"—Nussbaum nudged his fellow Daniel—"isn't that the little shrimp who kicked you in the face?"

Sanderson sat up and followed his pointing finger. "He's not so small. We're just high up, that's all."

I had to laugh. "Save my seat. I'm just going to run down for a minute and say hi to the team."

I worked my way through the crowd, which was made up mostly of parents and siblings of the contestants, mixed in with an assortment of teachers from the various participating schools. I stepped around a large cardboard sign that said GREAT NECK SOUTH ROBOTICS and jumped down to the floor. As I snaked through the grid of pits, I checked out a few robots. They were nothing special but, of course, I hadn't seen them in action yet.

I didn't know any of the contestants from other towns, but in a way they were familiar to me. They looked like the Academy kids. The brilliant dweebs, like Noah. The psycho overachievers, like Abigail. The hands-on engineers, like Latrell. The all-purpose brainiacs, like Chloe. There was even the occasional kid who reminded me of me—some average ungifted slob who happened to get taken along for the ride. Some of the teams were tinkering and fine-tuning; some were greeting old friends and competitors; a few pits had music playing—one group was dancing, doing "the robot."

*Right. We get it.*

The school banner read COLD SPRING HARBOR, but I would have known this team anywhere. Their pit was better equipped and better organized than anybody else's, from the easy-access tool rack to the stacked hammocks for relaxing between rounds. Their robot looked like it had just rolled off an assembly line in a high-tech factory. It had none of the homemade, cobbled-together appearance of Tin Man and most of the others. The shape reminded me of my grandma's giant stew pot if you added wheels and mechanical arms. But it was huge—Pot-zilla, Lord of the Robots.

Cold Spring Harbor were the defending champions, and the kids wore their arrogance like a uniform. Come to think of it, they had a real uniform—custom T-shirts that blazoned their achievements not just at this meet but at others around the country. To look at them was to want to ram their robot down their throats. But that might have been my team spirit. If my time in Oz's room had hammered one thing into my head, it was that Cold Spring Harbor was the enemy.

I passed Pot-zilla and headed down the narrow aisle for the Academy's pit, the smile already transforming my face. It had only been a week, but I could hardly believe how glad I felt at the prospect of seeing my former teammates again.

The smile didn't last. I was close—so close that I was about to call out to Oz—when a tall figure in a three-piece suit crossed my line of vision.

Schultz.

I did the fastest about-face in the history of direction changes. I couldn't let him see me! I was supposed to be in school right now! He'd had to let me off the hook for Atlas because it made him look bad too. But if he caught me here, cutting class to attend an event of the gifted program he'd just yanked me out of, I'd get no mercy.

I returned to the seats, heart pounding in my ears.

"Is it over yet?" Sanderson mumbled, half asleep.

"How are the dorks?" Katie asked fondly. "Do they look nervous?"

"They're fine," I assured her.

I wish I could have said the same thing about myself.

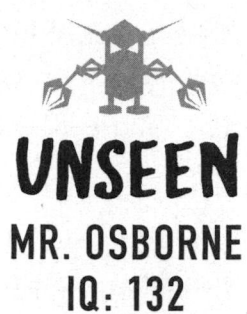

# UNSEEN

## MR. OSBORNE
## IQ: 132

The state robotics meet.

It was my favorite day of the year. There was nothing quite like it for our kids at the Academy. Schools have so many outlets for athletes to shine. But for the gifted program, robotics was ideal. It combined creativity, design, engineering, mechanics, electronics, pneumatics, and computer science, all in an atmosphere of healthy competition. It was sent from heaven.

This year? Not so much.

The team I brought to St. Leo was distracted and dispirited. And I hated to admit it, but I was too.

*He* should have been here. Donovan. And not just because he drove Tin Man better than anybody else. My group was unmatched in ability level, but it took Donovan to make them a team. On the surface, he contributed very little. But without him, nothing worked.

I should have been furious with that kid. He had committed an atrocious act of property damage. He had got into the gifted program under false pretenses, and had used it as an opportunity to hide from the consequences of his actions. He had cheated on the retest. Or, at minimum, he had let somebody cheat for him, which was even worse. He was barely from the same planet as my students.

If I had been a better teacher, I would have shouted down the class's complaints about Donovan's sudden departure from the Academy. When the bellyaching continued, I would have set a strict rule for our class: the name of Donovan Curtis was no longer to be mentioned within those walls. And if that hadn't worked, I would have told them a few home truths about misplaced loyalty, and people who lie and cheat to get their way. I had considered doing all those things. But I didn't. Because, deep down, I missed Donovan just as much as they did.

Maybe even more. I kept seeing him around the auditorium, as if wishful thinking might produce him in front of me. One time the illusion was so real that I actually began to wave before I looked again, and he wasn't there. That's the kind of impression the kid made.

Dr. Schultz shook my hand and nodded affably to the students. "Good luck, everybody. Make me proud."

If looks could have killed, he'd have been pinned to the wall by a volley of arrows. The last time they'd heard from their superintendent, he'd been pulling Donovan out of the gym, and out of their lives.

The first phase of the competition was the autodirected portion, where the robots navigate by electric eye, following a course of varicolored lines painted on the floor. By the time Tin Man's heat came up, Cold Spring Harbor was already in first place with a comfortable lead over Orchard Park in second. I watched, the team crouched around me, following the stopwatch in my hand, as Tin Man ran that course to perfection. My number was unofficial, of course, but I was certain our time was right up there with Cold

Spring Harbor's mechanical monster. And when the final scores went up, Tin Man Metallica Squarepants was ahead of the pack with a two-second lead over last year's champions. The performance held up, and we headed into phase two with a ten-point advantage.

We had a long break before our next event, and experience had taught me that that wasn't always a good thing, especially for front-runners. I tried to keep the kids busy, checking things that didn't need checking. But soon Noah came back from the bathroom with huge black thumbprints on the lenses of his glasses.

"What happened to you?" I asked anxiously. "Is that paint?"

"It was a stamp pad," he replied, annoyed and embarrassed. "Those Cold Spring Harbor guys did it to me. They were waiting in the bathroom."

I frowned. This was something you could expect from Cold Spring Harbor that you didn't get from any other team. They traveled with a large group, and two or three of them were big sullen boys who didn't seem to have much to do with their robot. I think they were there as intimidators. They had certainly done a pretty good job of intimidating Noah.

Abigail was angry. "We have to complain to the judges! They shouldn't get away with this!"

"Take it easy," I soothed, handing her a cup of YoukilAde. "They're just trying to get into our heads. And see? It's already worked. Forget about Cold Spring Harbor. We'll let Tin Man do our talking."

But as the competition progressed, the human element became a bigger factor. Abigail was at the controller, and she was darn good. But it was impossible to avoid comparisons with the way Donovan had handled the joystick. He couldn't make Tin Man go any faster, of course. But there was a nimbleness to his driving, an economy to the robot's maneuvers. Every cut and turn seemed to be an inch or two wider than it needed to be without Donovan at the helm. And all that extra motion added up to lost time. Before you knew it, Cold Spring Harbor had retaken the lead. Soon after that, we dropped to third position, and then fourth. That was a cause for worry, because if Tin Man fell one more place, we'd fail to qualify for the final round.

In the pit, we slaved over our robot. Noah ran a software diagnostic, and Latrell and Kevin agonized over each physical connection and bearing. We had to coax every microgram of performance out of Tin Man to keep our hopes alive.

I could see Abigail's fingers trembling as she worked the joystick. I can't say for sure if she was rattled before, but right now she was scared to death. I looked down at the stopwatch in my hand, and realized that I'd forgotten to start it. The atmosphere was that tense.

Tin Man had a big lead on the other three robots, but we knew that meant very little. None of the competition in this heat was battling us for that last spot in the finals. At this point, our opponent was the clock.

Tin Man reached the pole, and Abigail pressed the control to deploy the mini-bot. We held our breath as the magnet locked onto the metal of the pole. With a high-pitched whirring sound, the wheels engaged, and the small unit climbed the pole.

*Ding!* The bell sounded as the mini-bot reached the top.

The round was over, but the uncertainty had just begun. Had our time garnered enough points to keep us in the all-important fourth spot? Or had we dropped to fifth, out of the finals? We stood in a circle, holding hands and watching the scoreboard.

One by one, the names of the finalists began to appear.

1. Cold Spring Harbor
2. Orchard Park
3. Abercrombie Prep
4. Academy for Scholastic Distinction

We were in.

# UNCONTROLLED
## DONOVAN CURTIS
### IQ: 112

I leaped up out of my seat, fists punching at the air. *"Yeah! Go, Tin Man!"*

At that, I was several seconds behind the Daniels, who were whooping and high-fiving like madmen, drawing annoyed looks from the spectators around them. Even Katie, who was not much of an athlete these days, was on her feet, cheering.

I couldn't help wondering what it must have been like to be in the pit just then—all those guys going nuts as they got ready for the final contest. I could see Oz talking to Abigail, plotting strategy for the battle that lay ahead. She was the driver. Everything depended on her. I knew how it felt when the controller was in your hand.

The Daniels were analyzing the upcoming showdown like it was the pitching matchup for game seven of the World Series.

"Obviously, Tin Man is the best robot," Nussbaum expounded. "If he wasn't, we couldn't have won the autodirected competition."

"Yeah, but Cold Spring Harbor has been pulling further ahead of us every round," Sanderson worried. "If we can't pick up our driving, we're toast!"

Considering those guys had come to make fun of the parts of the meet they didn't sleep through, they seemed pretty involved in it now.

It took about twenty minutes to set up the grand finale, which involved having the robots place inflated rings of different sizes onto strategically placed pegs. It was the bread and butter of any meet, and we had practiced it endlessly. Each ring carried a different point value. Also, the round would be timed, with bonuses for early completion. It would be tough driving, but there was reason to be hopeful. You had to be constantly aware of what balance of speed and accuracy would get you the most points. A guy like Noah could spit out calculations like that faster than a computer.

A tense silence fell in the auditorium as the four robots were moved into their positions on the floor. Standing beside Cold Spring Harbor's gleaming Pot-zilla, poor Tin Man looked like a soapbox racer next to an Indy car. Albert Einstein's banana barely reached the lowest position of the front-runner's lifting arm. Tin Man *vs.* Pot-zilla; David *vs.* Goliath.

The whistle blew, and they were off. Chloe slipped a green ring around one of Tin Man's lifting forks, and our robot started across the course. The four competitors placed their first rings successfully, but Abercrombie Prep was beginning to fall behind as they came back for more.

"Let's go, Tin Man!" barked Sanderson.

"You can do it, dude!" Nussbaum added.

I held my breath when I saw the next ring. It was one of the black ones—small ring, small hole. Harder to handle, but with the highest point value. Orchard Park wasted precious seconds tightening a loose wheel. Tin Man lumbered back toward the pegs. The lift mechanism rose almost to its apex. It was going to be tricky—one false move, and that ring would hit the floor, taking the Academy's hopes with it.

The tiny ring found its place. The auditorium burst into applause, and Tin Man swung around for the next pass. Pot-zilla was hot on his heels, but with our hardest ring already in place, it was: advantage, Tin Man.

Our next ring was pink, the largest. That was when it happened. As Tin Man crossed the floor, Pot-zilla put on a sudden burst of speed. The swerve seemed completely natural, but it was just enough for one of the arms to sweep into Tin Man's path. It bumped lightly into the pink ring, knocking it off Tin Man's fork. It made no sound when it hit the floor, but it might as well have been a bomb blast.

A gasp went up in the auditorium.

"No-o-o-o!" chorused the Daniels.

Oz was on his feet, shouting at the judges, who were waving him off.

Abigail was panicking, fumbling to pick up the dropped ring. Pot-zilla motored past. Soon after, Orchard Park and Abercrombie followed.

I jumped up. "That was on purpose!"

Katie shot me a sharp look. "Donnie, don't you dare!"

But I was already running. I don't know what I

thought I could accomplish. At minimum, I had to calm Abigail down, talk her through the operation of picking up the fallen ring, get everything back on track.

I pounded down the stairs, and leaped to the floor.

Chloe was the first to notice me. "Donovan?"

One by one, the team members recognized me. Faces lit up. Cries of greeting rang out. But this was no time for a reunion. Our chance of winning the robotics meet was slipping away with every tick of the clock.

"Donovan!" Abigail was last. Her eyes were huge, her expression desperate.

I started shouting instructions, struggling for calm myself. "Take the joystick and—"

She had a better idea. She thrust the controller into my hands, and backed away, panting.

What could I do? I lowered the lift mechanism, tipped up the ring and skewered it with one of the forks. Then I delivered it to its destination, deftly raising it, and placing it onto the peg.

Wasting no time, I wheeled Tin Man around and headed back toward Chloe. She looked devastated, shaking her head tragically. I understood the message instantly. I was too late. Pot-zilla had already picked up the final ring and was headed toward the peg and victory.

I saw red. After sabotaging us, Cold Spring Harbor was *not* going home with first prize. Not while I had the joystick in my hand. I drove Tin Man right into the path of the big shiny pot.

"Donovan!" shouted Oz. *"Stop!"*

Pot-zilla was bigger and heavier, but Cold Spring Harbor didn't know that Tin Man had a secret weapon—a powerful motor in the lift mechanism, one that had polished every floor in the Academy for Scholastic Distinction.

A split second before impact, I engaged the forklift. Tin Man picked up Pot-zilla bodily, the larger robot's Mecanum wheels spinning without traction.

Absolute pandemonium broke out. The Cold Spring Harbor kids were screaming, but my team was matching them in volume. The head judge was blowing his whistle, but it could not be heard over the general din. Neither could Schultz, who was shouting at me from behind Chloe. Anyway, I couldn't stop now. Tin Man was a bundle of circuits, incapable of revenge fantasy, but I was all too human.

Cold Spring Harbor's driver was trying to free Pot-zilla by thrashing with its lifting arms. I needed to act fast. Tin Man had been designed for competition, not combat, so I had to improvise a little. I swiveled ninety degrees and, using Pot-zilla as a battering ram, I charged the scorer's table.

Oz hollered, *"Do-o-o-on-o-o-o-va-a-an!"* It came out a ten-syllable word.

But I was committed. The judges scrambled for cover as I slammed that big pot right into the steel-reinforced corner of the table. Pot-zilla bounced off, dented. One lifting arm hung limply by its shiny bulk. The other reached for Tin Man with evil intent. I backed my robot away.

A shriek behind me penetrated even the chaotic noise of the crowd. Noah bounded onto the scene. He snatched up one of the judges' abandoned chairs, and brought it down, WWE style, on Pot-zilla's polished crown.

*Wham!* And then again. *Wham! Wham! Wham!*

If the cybernetic pot hadn't been finished before, it was finished now. It wobbled once, and keeled over, lying there, an upended cockroach, wheels turning like struggling legs.

The auditorium had been rocking with excitement, dismay, horror, laughter, and outrage. But now that the action seemed to be over, a strange hush fell as people waited to see what would happen next. Considering the craziness of the situation, it was a strangely familiar moment to me. The impulsive act was over, but the consequences had not yet descended on my head. It was as if time had ground to a halt, and we were all frozen there. What the future held I couldn't predict, but I had a sense that it had something to do with Dr. Schultz, pushing through the throng toward me, his face a thundercloud.

A high-pitched voice suddenly cut through the eerie silence. *"Donnie—"* It was Katie, struggling down the grandstand steps. *"Donnie—it's time!"*

I was so wrapped up in the insanity that I wasn't thinking straight. "Time for what?"

Chloe wasn't like me. She was in the gifted program for real. "The baby!" she exclaimed. "Katie's having the baby!"

# UNEXPECTED
## CHLOE GARFINKLE
## IQ: 159

*<<Hypothesis: The speed of the drive is directly proportional to the acuteness of the crisis.>>*

The yellow minibus squealed up to the emergency entrance of St. Leo Medical Center, and the disqualified Academy robotics team piled out, bearing Katie Patterson with us. While Oz and Donovan handled the patient registration, Katie and the rest of us lay on the waiting-room carpet, practicing Noah's breathing technique.

"Don't worry," Katie assured the two bewildered Daniels. "This pregnancy is a group effort."

"Cool," said the taller one, but he looked a little unnerved.

A door swung open, and an orderly appeared, pushing a wheelchair. "Mrs. Patter"—he gawked at us on the floor—"what's going on down there?"

"It's okay," Latrell told him. "We're the birthing team!"

"We only do robotics in our spare time," Noah explained.

Katie was loaded into the chair and brought to a case room. We followed, every last one of us. The staff wasn't too keen on that, but they had no choice. We were all her coaches, except for the Daniels, and they kept their mouths shut for a change. I'd never seen them so well behaved.

We were in there forever, breathing and timing contractions with our robotics stopwatch. We studied the final sonogram, and kept a close eye on the fetal heart monitor that Katie wore. Everything was fine, but Donovan seemed really scared, even more than his sister, and she was the one having the baby. He spent most of the time on the phone, trying to locate his parents to let them know what was going on. We all took turns calling home to inform our families that this robotics meet was going on a lot longer than usual.

Finally, the doctor decided it was time to take his patient into delivery. As the brother, Donovan went too. The rest of us congregated in the waiting room to—well—wait.

You could tell the two Daniels were pretty cowed by the whole adventure.

"So is this, like, business as usual for the gifted program?" the taller one asked. "I mean, do you do this kind of stuff a lot?"

Oz favored him with an exhausted chuckle. "You mean trash a robotics meet and have a baby? No. It's fair to say this is a big day even for us."

"What's going to happen to us?" Abigail wondered anxiously. "Do you think we might be banned from future competition?"

Oz shrugged miserably. "I don't know. Interfering with another robot is a very serious offense. There are bound to be consequences."

"It was worth it!" the shorter Daniel exploded. "I've known Donovan since first grade, and that was him at his best! Real gladiator stuff!"

"It was WWE," Noah amended.

"You were great too, kid," the other Daniel assured

him. "Mess with you and pay the price. I learned the hard way."

I spoke up. "What Donovan did was against the rules, but it was *right*. Cold Spring Harbor interfered with our robot before he interfered with theirs."

Our teacher sighed. "That's assuming the judges noticed. If they didn't, they'll see the attack as unprovoked."

"But effective," Noah put in.

Kevin rubbed his hands together. "It was beautiful to see that tin pot with a big dent in it."

"I was hoping the arm would fall off," Latrell added wistfully.

"Well, they definitely didn't deserve to win," Abigail said reluctantly. "Even if that means we can't win either."

Jacey opened her mouth to speak, and I braced for one of her odd random comments. Instead, she said softly but with conviction, "Way to go, Donovan."

It hit me just then how different we all were since Donovan had been mistakenly sent to the Academy. The mayhem that had ended the robotics meet would have freaked us out a few weeks ago. Now we were gloating over having destroyed our enemy. If Oz had hoped Donovan would become more like us, here was proof that the opposite was true. *We* had become more like Donovan.

I love my school, but I'd always yearned for us to be a little more normal.

<<*Hypothesis: Today we finally got there.*>>

We'd been cooling our heels for about an hour when Dr. Schultz came into the waiting room. The superintendent's hair was wild, his tie undone, his normally immaculate suit rumpled.

Spying us, he rushed over. "Any news?"

"Nothing yet," Oz informed him.

He looked frazzled. "I've got your robot in the trunk of my car, but the rest of your equipment is in the storage room at the auditorium. All except the YoukilAde. That got spilled out in the . . . confusion."

"What did the judges finally decide?" asked Oz, and I could tell he wasn't sure he wanted to hear the answer.

"You were disqualified and so was Cold Spring Harbor," the superintendent reported. "Orchard Park were the winners, but I don't think that means much this year. The whole thing was a major fiasco. This is supposed to be a friendly science competition, not a gang rumble."

"Are we in really big trouble?" Abigail asked in a small voice.

"I'm honestly not sure," replied Dr. Schultz. "I inquired several times, but no one would give me a straight answer. The judges have never dealt with this kind of misconduct before. That might work in our favor."

"We should probably keep a low profile in the robotics association for a while," Oz suggested, and we all chimed in our agreement.

Low profile or not, this was one robotics meet I'd never forget. The image of Donovan working the joystick, exacting Tin Man's revenge, would forever be burned onto the inside of my eyelids. I'll bet the others—even Abigail—felt the same way.

<<Hypothesis: *To take a robot designed to place rings on pegs and turn it into an instrument of destruction requires a kind of giftedness that none of us have.*>>

It was then that the heavy swinging door was flung wide and Donovan staggered out to the waiting room, wide-eyed and white-faced. He was quite a sight in green scrubs and a surgical cap. "It happened," he rasped.

"And?" I prompted eagerly.

"It's a girl," he managed. "Katie had a baby girl!"

The waiting room erupted in cheers and we mobbed him with backslaps and congratulations.

<<Hypothesis: *!!!!!!*>>

Okay, that wasn't a hypothesis. It was just awesome.

"Dude, you're an uncle!" the taller Daniel exclaimed. "You did it!"

"*Katie* did it," I amended. I threw my arms around Donovan and gave him a big hug.

He seemed startled, and I admit it was a little closer than any of the others got. But I was just so happy for Katie. I *knew* the day Donovan stepped into the robotics lab that there were great things ahead. And this was the greatest of them all.

Donovan worked his way through the well-wishers and nearly jumped out of his scrubs at the sight of Dr. Schultz.

"You can't blame Donovan," I jumped in. "Cold Spring Harbor started it."

The entire team burst into a babbling description of how our opponents deliberately knocked the ring out of Tin Man's control.

"I couldn't let them beat us," Donovan finished. "Not that way."

"I don't appreciate rule breaking," the superintendent said gravely. "School spirit, however, is something I appreciate very much. Whatever else you are, Donovan Curtis, you're a loyal teammate." He smiled. "And please pass on my congratulations to your sister, her husband, and their new daughter."

"Wait a minute!" Noah's brow furrowed. "It can't be a daughter. The sonogram clearly showed a boy."

Oz laughed. "Well, I guess you were wrong about that."

The look on Noah's face as he took in the enormity of that statement was sheer wonder. "Wrong . . ." he repeated, dazed. "I was . . . wrong."

"It's no big deal, Noah," I told him gently.

"It's a colossal deal. I'm *never* wrong." All at once, his normally serious expression dissolved into a large goofy grin. "This is the greatest moment of my life!"

"Maybe, if you get really lucky, you can be wrong again someday," Donovan teased.

Noah considered this. "I'll work on it in summer school."

"No, you won't." Oz was jubilant. "This class was short fourteen hours of Human Growth and Development instruction. But remember, real-life experience counts as triple time."

I snapped to attention. "We've been with Katie four hours already. One more hour and—"

A flicker of hope animated Abigail's features. "No summer school?"

Dr. Schultz smiled. "Perhaps some good has actually

come out of this horrendous experience. I will personally sign your credit."

"But we have to put in the final hour," Oz added.

"I wouldn't leave anyway," I announced. "Not till I've seen our baby!"

<<*Hypothesis: Maybe the Human Growth and Development requirement isn't so pointless after all.*>>

# UNBURDENED
## ABIGAIL LEE
## IQ: 171

I refuse to let this mess leave a hole in my record.

I spent hours, days even, trying to draft the perfect line to take credit for being on the robotics team without taking blame for what the robotics team had done. *Disqualified* was such an ugly word; *banned* was even worse. *Conduct unbecoming a scientist*—no, don't even go there.

I finally went with: *2012 State Robotics Meet, First-Place Power Ranking (DNF)*. Maybe no one would look into the definition of DNF (Did Not Finish), or realize that there was no such thing as a first-place power ranking—which just meant that our robot beat the snot out of Cold Spring Harbor's robot. I don't think Harvard's admissions department would be too impressed by that. It wouldn't hurt someone like Noah. He would get into college wherever he wanted. Sadly, he would probably go nowhere at all. I never thought I'd say this: There was such a thing as being too smart. Confession: I was jealous of Noah. I'd give anything to spend an hour inside his head, to take a mind like that out for a test drive. But I wouldn't want to be him—even though he'd always be above a black mark like the robotics meet, which would be an Ivy League deal breaker for the rest of us.

Another thing Harvard could never be allowed to find out about: how close I came to going to summer school for Human Growth and Development. Do you think their admissions department would care that it wasn't my fault? Of course not. Everybody knows who goes to summer school: People who can't pass in the fall, winter, and spring. People who actually have to open up their report cards to find out their grades. People who think a Rhodes scholarship is Driver's Ed. At least I'd been spared *that* black mark—thanks to Donovan Curtis.

Yes, I know I was really hard on Donovan, and said a lot of terrible things about him. And I stand by my original opinion that he never should have been in the gifted program. But that doesn't mean that we all weren't really lucky for the Atlas incident that put him in Oz's class.

Which brings up the final piece of information that Harvard could never be permitted to learn. Ditto Yale, Princeton, Columbia, Brown, Dartmouth, Stanford, Penn, and Cornell. If anyone accuses me of this, I'll deny it. I might even sue.

I was the one who hacked into the library computer and helped Donovan cheat on the retest.

Surprised?

Me too.

# UNCHALLENGED
## NOAH YOUKILIS
## IQ: 206

I'm not sure how the clip made it to YouTube.

The organizers said that the official video of this year's state meet would never be released because our "disgraceful thuggish behavior degraded school robotics programs everywhere."

Somehow, though, the video of Tin Man vanquishing the competition appeared the very next day under the title "Robots Behaving Badly."

I would have called it "The Second-Most Fantastically

Awesome Blow for Justice Ever Struck by an Automaton (after the Terminator Turned Good)." But that might have been too long. People on YouTube don't want to *read*; they want to *watch*. You have to keep it simple to generate traffic. Example: "Robots Behaving Badly" had already surpassed "Tin Man Metallica Squarepants Exposes Teacher's Underwear" in barely a week online.

I felt a little insulted that this new clip had so easily bested my most popular video. But it was okay, since I was the costar of "Robots Behaving Badly," bounding onto the scene at the end to beat the Cold Spring Harbor entry into submission with a folding chair.

It was a great action sequence, every bit as exciting as the real steel-chair battles in WWE videos. I could be wrong, though.

After all, I've been wrong before.

The old-fashioned dot-matrix printer in the main office made a screeching noise as it spat out my class schedule. It sounded like victory. The secretary tore off the page and placed it on the counter along with my student card and locker information.

She smiled at me. "New in town?"

"I've lived here all my life," I told her. "It just took

me this long to get thrown out of the gifted program."

This great day never could have happened if I hadn't been wrong about the sex of Katie Patterson's baby. Just the thought that when I calculate, interpolate, extrapolate, infer, deduce, adjudge, analyze, derive, figure, reason, or surmise something, there's a chance that I might not be right filled me with a sense of infinite possibility. Surprise didn't come exclusively from YouTube anymore. It was a gift.

I owed this, too, to Donovan. Without him, I never would have crossed paths with Tina Mandy Patterson, seven pounds, fourteen ounces. I'd suggested Marie Curie Patterson, but Katie said no. Tina would be named after the star of the day of her birth—Tin Man.

I pointed out that, since Tin Man had been disqualified, he wasn't technically the star of the robotics meet or anything else. But Katie overruled me. And anyway, Orchard Park Patterson was a really stupid name for a baby girl.

I'm not big on babies, but I had to admit that Tina was a very cute specimen of one. Subscribe to my YouTube channel to see what she looks like. There's a clip of her spitting up on my shoes that's particularly excellent. It's my favorite because I got to hold her.

Katie gave each of us a turn so long as we promised to wash our hands for three minutes uninterrupted. One minute would have been plenty given the strength of the antibacterial soap in the maternity ward, but I kept my mouth shut because I didn't want to miss my chance.

Chloe got in trouble for hogging the baby.

I thanked the secretary, gathered my things, and left the office.

*I was wrong.* It still tickled me to think about it. And for sure that's what had given me the confidence to do what needed to be done to make this glorious moment possible.

*"Noah?"* came a voice behind me in the hall.

I wheeled, and there he was, the author of all my good fortune. My former schoolmate and now my schoolmate again.

Donovan. "What are you doing here?" he asked.

I felt my chest swell with pride. "This is my new school."

He was shocked. "They kicked you out of the Academy? Because of the chair?"

"Oh, no," I replied. "They didn't even mention that. It was because I helped you cheat on the retest."

First he looked surprised, then angry. "I knew it! If you weren't a genius, you'd be an idiot! You shouldn't have done that, Noah! I wasn't going to be able to hang on in there much longer anyway, test or no test. Why would you risk your whole school career to cheat for me?"

"I didn't," I informed him cheerfully. "I just *said* I did."

His voice was rising. "But why?"

"Ms. Bevelaqua told me cheating was a serious offense, and whoever did it would be expelled. How could I pass up an opportunity like that?"

Donovan groaned. "You're crazy. And the worst part is, now I'm never going to know who really did it."

I shrugged. "Sure you are. It was Abigail."

"No way!" His eyes bulged. "Abigail hated me from the first day I walked into the lab! Why would she help me?"

It's strange to me how often I have to explain the obvious to people. "For your robot-driving skills and your sister. Abigail has always been about one thing— Abigail."

"I don't believe it," Donovan said stubbornly.

"Believe it," I recommended. "I had to erase all the

computer evidence that she did it when I created the fake evidence that *I* did it."

He took this in with a mixture of amazement and resignation. "You're crazy."

"I don't care," I replied readily. "See, now that I go here, I can say that. Who cares? Not me! I could not possibly care less! What do I care?" It felt good, like I was unburdening myself of a great weight.

He heaved a sigh. "Well, congratulations, I guess. You got your wish. You managed to get yourself booted out of the only school with half a chance of challenging you."

I was honest. "The Academy wasn't very challenging either."

"More challenging than here," he shot back. "This place is a slumber party for a guy like you. Maybe even a morgue."

I shook my head earnestly. "I was *wrong* about Katie's baby, and that means I can be wrong about anything. Challenge isn't going to come from any curriculum, no matter how hard they make it. It's going to come from life."

That sounded pretty good, even to me. I felt the exhilaration of facing the unknown. I wasn't just heading into the future; I was taking it down, WWE-style. I was Noah Youkilis, version 2.0, and the best was yet to come!

Then again, I could always be wrong.

How awesome was that?

# UNLITTERED
## DONOVAN CURTIS
## IQ: 112

The image was fuzzy at first. Noah pounded the keyboard of his laptop and the picture solidified into a rugged face, obscured by goggles, a chinstrap, and a heavy black helmet. Interference crackled over the audio, and a loud motor roared in the background.

"Lieutenant Patterson?" Noah ventured timidly. Louder: "Lieutenant Patterson?"

My brother-in-law looked around in confusion.

"Who's saying that?"

Another member of the tank crew came into view, pointing out at us. "Look, Brad, it's that kid from YouTube! The one your baby puked on!"

Noah seemed pleased to be recognized. "Nice tank. How's Afghanistan?"

"Brad, it's Donovan," I piped up. "We've got something to show you."

Brad squinted through the goggles. "Is Katie there? Is it happening?"

Katie leaned in front of the laptop. "Hi, Brad. It won't be long now."

The tank commander was excited. "Turn the computer! I want to watch!"

Noah swiveled the laptop, giving Brad a view of the sterile white walls of the clinic, and also of Chloe, Abigail, Latrell, Jacey, and Kevin. At last, the image stopped on Dr. Orsini in his surgical mask.

The other soldier opened his eyes wide. "What's going on, Brad? Didn't this happen last week? Don't tell me they're going back in for the twin they missed!"

Noah made a final adjustment, providing a view of the patient—Beatrice the chow chow, fat and round, about to litter.

"Beatrice!" Brad cried, his voice choked with

emotion. "It's Daddy! Hang in there, girl!"

And as his tank jounced along the Afghan terrain, Lieutenant Patterson watched, tears squeezing out from under the goggles, as his beloved pet deposited six tiny puppies onto the operating table. Compared to the four hours Katie had spent in labor, Beatrice had it easy: The whole thing was over in ninety seconds.

"They make dogs really fast," commented Noah.

"They're beautiful, Brad," said Katie in a husky voice. "You missed Tina being born, but I'm so glad you got to see these little guys."

Noah spoke into the laptop's condenser mic. "Your signal is getting weaker. Are you near a mountain or something?"

"That's classified, kid," Brad replied. "I don't know who you are, but I owe you. Anybody who can Skype a tank in action has really got it going on."

"And I loved you in 'Robots Behaving Badly,'" the other soldier added admiringly.

Then, with a burst of static, Afghanistan went dark.

"Transmission lost," Noah reported. "Should I hack into another satellite?"

"No," Katie decided. "Leave them alone. They're working."

That was how our Human Growth and Development class turned into Canine Growth and Development— at least for one afternoon. The decision was made to keep a puppy for baby Tina, and find good homes for the others. Chloe adopted one dog. I was kind of glad about that. It gave me an excuse to stay in touch with her—you know, just to keep an eye on how Beatrice's kid was getting along.

Noah fit in better than I expected at Hardcastle Middle School. Some of that might have been because I recruited the Daniels, and the three of us formed a bodyguard unit to keep him from being wedgied to death. Who knows what would have happened without us. We liked him, and Sanderson was convinced he was a master of "Dorkido," a secret martial art practiced only by geniuses. But Noah *was* the biggest dweeb who'd ever walked the face of the earth. And while he insisted he could be wrong again at any moment, it hadn't happened so far.

By special request from Oz, both Noah and I traveled by minibus to the Academy three times a week for robotics. The plan was approved by Dr. Schultz himself, who was in a good mood because the insurance company had finally paid up and the gym was being repaired. What was left of Atlas had joined its celestial sphere in the administration building's sub-basement. I hoped I didn't have to polish that piece too. I still had five and half hours of community service to go.

Dr. Schultz had put boxes in all the schools, soliciting suggestions for a new statue. I filled out a card for a *Titanic* memorial—a quiet nod to my ancestor and fellow survivor, James.

Noah didn't mind spending a little time back at the Academy because I was going too. And I loved the change of scenery, and the chance to hang out and ply my joystick in the lab. I never confronted Abigail about how she had cheated for me on the retest. She definitely still hated me, but I had a sense that my reading on her personal grudge-o-meter had gone down a little. Maybe she was more comfortable now that all the cards were on the table. She was still smart, and I was officially ungifted—except for robotics, part-time.

We were working on Heavy Metal, our robot for next year's competition. We'd be in the high school division then, and hopefully no one would remember whose entry had busted up the middle school meet. Tin Man's rampage would live forever in infamy, but maybe the team behind him would fade into the background. Soon the riot would belong to Tin Man alone, and all that remained would be the question, What made the robot go berserk like that?

Hey, I had *that* answer. It was the same wild impulse that could make a guy whack a statue in the butt, setting off a chain of events that reshaped the world—or at least my little corner of it. It was the part of me that ancestry.com couldn't explain. I was working to control it, but sooner or later it would show up again and get me into twice as much trouble.

You don't have to be gifted to know that.

# GORDON KORMAN

has written more than seventy middle-grade and teen novels. Favorites include the *New York Times* bestselling *The 39 Clues: Cahills vs. Vespers Book One: The Medusa Plot*; *Pop*; *Schooled*; *No More Dead Dogs*; *Son of the Mob*; and *Born to Rock*. Gordon lives with his family on Long Island, New York. You can visit him online at www.gordonkorman.com.